Sign up for our newsletter to hear
about new and upcoming releases.

www.ylva-publishing.com

the pond

CHERI CRYSTAL

Dedicated with love and gratitude to three of
the most important women in my life:

Marilyn Crystal
Jo Gregson
Sara Rosenberg

Acknowlegements

Across the Pond would still be in the revision stage if it hadn't been for the collective efforts of many who helped along the way. I could not have done it without their support.

With gratitude, I thank my publisher, Astrid Ohletz, for believing in me and for all her encouragement, expertise, and hard work. I'm especially grateful to her for granting my stories a warm and cozy den. It's a privilege being a part of the Ylva pack.

I must also thank Ylva's senior editor, Sandra Gerth, for sharing her brilliant mind via Skype and email, because a brain chip simply isn't available.

To my amazing editor, Michelle Aguilar, I appreciate her for showing me the way to making *Across the Pond* what it is today. She made the editing process virtually painless, even when I had to delete a few scenes I didn't think my story could live without. With her professional help, it's a much better book. I thank her for that!

I also thank my gifted cover artist, Glendon Haddix, for an incredible job. He makes me proud to have my name on such a good-looking cover.

If not for my generous beta readers, whose input inspired me to improve my story and to finally put it out there, I might not have submitted it for publication. I owe them all a huge debt of gratitude for generously reading the numerous versions without too much complaint. What can I say? They rock! And they know who they are.

I'm indebted to Joey Bass for tirelessly listening while I read the manuscript aloud multiple times. I thank her for keeping me company on those rainy days in Devon—when I was only too happy to stay put—and for making so many useful suggestions.

To Clare I grant a million thanks for commenting on romantic fiction, even though she much prefers reading non-fiction—particularly science, no less!

I thank Mie for lending a younger woman's perspective and for providing such excellent feedback. Her thoughts have been useful, insightful, and much appreciated.

To my writing coach Toni Amato who taught me lots about writing as a craft and not just a hobby. I simply can't thank him enough.

To my mom I offer a huge helping of gratitude for everything. I thank her for sharing her honest opinion, whether I ask for it or not. I love and appreciate her to no end.

To my incredible children Brian, Eric, and Sara, who support me in all that I do and who make me extremely happy, proud, and grateful to be their mother. I love them more than life!

To Jo—my wife, my love, my life—I thank her for all she says and does. Even her nagging proves her undying devotion. I love her with all my heart.

Chapter 1

Autumn to Winter 2008

IT DIDN'T TAKE MUCH TO excite me, not like I was ridiculously easy to please, but happiness came from within. I was animated because I loved surprises, especially when I was the one behind them. My bliss had me dirty dancing with a wooden spoon one minute, hip-hopping and flailing around a spatula the next, and twirling a potato masher to a disco beat, until I was burning calories like a well-oiled furnace. It was a good thing too, because I was cooking up a special dinner to commemorate our thirteenth anniversary. Thirteen! Our lucky number, but still hard to believe it had been that long since Faith and I had first met at a *Mostly Mozart* orchestra concert at Lincoln Center. Her tastes in music had done a complete turnaround from the classical she had preferred back then. These days she was a fanatic for anything Latin American, and the spicier the salsa, the better. While I enjoyed everything from country to glam rock, she sure did adore the Latin beat, and it was growing on me too.

She'd be home soon. I had great plans of spending quality time with her. And yes, I had high hopes to spend most of that quality time with her in bed. Both our jobs seriously cut into our cuddle time. Faith saved struggling restaurants from bankruptcy, and I helped motivate employees toward healthier lifestyle choices in order to cut absenteeism and increase productivity. Tonight, I planned to make up for all the time we'd had to spend apart recently.

I'd taken time off today to mark the occasion and even treated myself to a decadent spa treatment—from a brand-new hairdo, mani, pedi and facial to a full leg and Brazilian bikini wax. It wasn't every day I went to great pains, literally, to look my best, being more of the rustic type in tune with what Mother Nature gave me. But the results had been miraculous: As soon as the tortuous tingles of pulling hairs out by the roots had subsided, I sparkled all over.

The table was pure elegance: I set it with our best china and stemware, placed matches alongside the decorative candles, and chilled the champagne in an ice bucket. A whole sustainable salmon was slow-roasting in the oven. Already I could detect a hint of delicate seasonings in the air. By the time it was done, the skin would be crispy, the pink meat beneath moist and succulent, and the buttery orange glaze would be fragrant and delicious. And Faith, my love, would be in culinary heaven.

As soon as I heard tires crunching and kicking up gravel, the buzz I'd had all day grew stronger. I knew how much my girl loved being catered to and just how high her standards were when it came to the taste and presentation of food. And pleasing her was one of my greatest joys. Diverting my attention away from the pile of freshly scrubbed and peeled vegetables, I placed my paring knife on the cutting board, moved the curtain aside with my clean knuckle, and glanced out the window. Our remodeled driveway, not yet tarmacked, wrapped around the side of the house where it led to the back garden. We could throw a huge party and invite a house-load of guests with room to spare if we were so inclined. But Faith was not a fan of parties, and I was mostly glad to have just two cars out there. Hers and mine—side by side.

Sure enough, Faith was home. My heart beat faster. Before she powered the windows up, I received an earful of Ricky Martin's "Livin' la Vida Loca." Both music and engine quit in sync as Faith cut the ignition of her brand-new red Toyota Camry. She strode toward the front of the house, uniform grey pebbles parting like the Red Sea as she went. The convenient side door was bolted shut until we were ready to build a staircase that was safe to navigate. Faith was chief-in-charge of home repairs and had promised months ago she'd get around to it, but she hadn't as of yet.

No matter how many times we sprayed the lock with WD-40, she'd no-doubt struggle with the key. If I nagged her to fix something or call someone in, we'd only argue, so I always let it go, and would again today. There were more important things on my mind: the sooner she stepped inside, the quicker we could get the party started, and the happier I'd be.

My first inclination whenever Faith arrived home was to run into her arms. But after she'd put in a sixty-hour week plus a grueling commute from anywhere in the Tri-State Area to Eastern Long Island during the Friday evening rush hour, I knew better than to invade her space the second she crossed the threshold. Although I got grouchy waiting, I considered allowing her to chill and greet me on her own terms a small sacrifice to pay. I'd finish up in the kitchen, and she'd walk in to find me all smiles.

With my heart rate mounting in direct proportion to my anticipation, I wiped my hands on the full-length apron I wore to protect my dress. It made me glance down at my clothing choice, and I realized I wasn't too upset to wear the dress again, after a shopping trip had failed to turn up a better alternative. I hoped Faith would be pleased at me choosing her favorite, a sheer number in deep plum with outlines of butterflies, buds, and leaves in cream; she'd bought it for me while on one of her business trips. It had a built-in, flesh-colored slip, hinting at the allusion of being bare but with a modicum of modesty. Only, on this special occasion, I had nothing on underneath. Without undergarments, this totally nice dress turned naughty. Maybe it was the feel of silk over freshly waxed skin, but I felt so sexy, mere walking threatened to bring me to the brink of orgasm.

I'd have come where I stood if not for a tactic that usually worked to quell unwanted passions best saved for later: I tried forcing my mind to imagine myself at the gym in a spinning class, the most unsexy thing I could think of. However, even that couldn't stop me from reliving old memories of Faith ripping this dress off and having her way with me in all sorts of kinky delights on the kitchen floor. I kept fast-forwarding to having all of her in bed tonight.

Speaking of Faith…it seemed to take ages for her to appear. The time it took her to place her shoulder bag and keys on the console table in the entryway, set her briefcase beside the hall closet, and drape her coat over the high-backed chair in the living room was often enough for her to unwind before entering the kitchen ready for a welcome embrace. Not crowding her earned me tons of sweet rewards.

It was a routine that ultimately suited us both. However, this was not an ordinary night for typical routines; it was our anniversary. Only, Faith hadn't mentioned a word about it all week, despite several of my not-so-subtle hints.

If I scrubbed the carrots any harder, they would be pared without a peeler.

I basted the fish again, mostly to have something to do with my restless hands, and then resumed stirring the cheese sauce on top of the stove. With assorted vegetables in a rainbow of colors all lined up, I reached over to the windowsill and switched tracks from dance to romance. Faith might tease me about altering the words to every sappy tune I'd ever heard, but I didn't care. Soon the first floor of our house was filled with the sounds of love songs, nothing but love songs, with me the lead vocalist—singing at the top of my lungs and jazzing up lyrics to my heart's content.

From a very early age, I could be counted on to burst into song on cue. Often I wasn't even aware I was humming until I was ordered to stop. Like my dad, I simply loved music. Did my mother have a premonition when she named me Janalyn Melody Jacobs? Or did I enjoy singing as a result of my middle name? But I liked to think I sang on-key, even if I could never remember the lyrics. I used to assume a line in "God Bless America" went "...from the night with the light from a bulb." I've since learned the error of my ways, but I continued to sing it my way just to make a point. After being ostracized by one's critical fourth grade peers for being different, I'd learned early that some battles weren't worth fighting. Let them make fun. If worse came to worst I could always just beat them up. I never did use my fists, but the thought I could went a long way to getting me through those awkward teens.

Back then I enjoyed creating silly medleys, not caring if they made sense or not, and now I couldn't be bothered to memorize actual lyrics. With my back to the door, I tore three varieties of lettuce leaves, slicing cucumbers, zucchini, celery stalks, radishes, scallions, tomato wedges, and four colors of peppers and tossed them all into a salad. Dried cranberries, caramelized pecans and crumbled feta cheese went on top for an extra zing. I was singing a borrowed tune from the song du jour rattling around in my head, singing, "hey you sexy thing, dah, duh, dah, duh, get down and dirty and let's have a fling, dah duh, dah, dah—" when Faith tapped my shoulder, startling me half to death, sending me nearly to the moon.

"A *fling*? Faith grasped her chest as if fatally wounded in the old country and western film style.

I turned to face her, blushing at first before putting on a deadpan expression. "If that's your interpretation of taking your last breath, then you mustn't quit your day job."

Unable to keep a straight face for long, I burst into laughter. She was much better at bluffing than me. It was a nuisance being unable to hide my emotions. It was no surprise she was great at poker, often beating the pants off me—literally.

"So, what about this fling you're having in our kitchen?" Faith said with an overly pronounced pout.

"*Fling* rhymes with *thing*. Need I say more dar*ling*, dah, duh, dah, duh?"

She rolled her eyes before I threw my arms around her neck, unable to stand another second without a proper greeting.

After thirteen years, my heart rate still sped up whenever she walked into a room, and heaven help my libido if she merely glanced my way; I was a goner then. I placed tiny kisses all over her face, lingering at her lips, only stopping to say what was in my heart: "Who needs a fling when I have you?"

Faith chuckled and ran the fingers of her free hand through my hair. "Hello, beautiful. Oh my, somebody changed her hairstyle."

I bit my bottom lip. "Do you like it?"

"I love it, and I love you too."

I shivered with delight whenever she paid extra attention to my appearance. She was my aphrodisiac. I was so absorbed in her presence; it took a while to notice that she was artfully keeping her other hand behind her back. With an overactive inquisitive nature, I stood on tiptoes to peer over her shoulder at what lay in wait for me to discover, but she blocked my view.

"No fair!" All I could detect over the pungent aroma of exotic spices that clung to her hair and clothing was a definite scent of fruit salad—a melon and strawberry patch and a pineapple grove smothered in chocolate. She radiated with obvious delight, a mischievous twinkle in her gray eyes.

"What did you bring me? Please let me see." I went to grab for it but was thwarted again. Faith was an expert at suspense. Possibly another of her appealing qualities, but I wasn't telling her that.

"Now may I please see my present?"

"May I have another kiss first?"

"For you, there's an unlimited supply." I placed my lips on hers and was deeply rewarded with the grand welcome to which I was accustomed.

I returned the favor and ran my fingers through her hair, gingerly massaging her scalp with my fingertips, while she closed her eyes, as if allowing her tense neck muscles to fully relax, one fiber at a time, until I was practically supporting her head and she was putty in my hands. I marveled at the potpourri of sights, scents and sounds that made up the whole of my girl. Faith was a conglomeration in many ways: outspoken yet reserved; tough as nails but a total mush; super-smart but not conceited. And while she came across as somewhat prudish to the outside world, she was sexy as hell in the bedroom. The many sides of Faith intrigued me to no end because I got to appreciate the real her.

I could have lingered this way for the remainder of the evening but my bionic nose just wouldn't let me forget: "Show me my present already, or I shall have to tickle you without mercy," I said.

With a flourish and a great big smile, Faith whipped out a tremendous fresh fruit bouquet from behind her back. I gasped at how the colorful arrangement of fresh fruit: cantaloupe, honeydew, strawberries, pineapple-shaped flowers—some naked and others cloaked in chocolate—formed an incredible bouquet. A rectangle slice of dark chocolate, held up by a plastic stand, had pink-icing letters inside a big red heart drawn on it—*F and J Forever*.

"Happy anniversary, Janalyn."

I held the bouquet to my nose and inhaled the sweetness. "This will be the perfect dessert, after the main dessert we're having in bed." I winked.

"Perfect. Did you by any chance make salmon?"

"A whole salmon."

"Oh, yum." Another thing I admired about Faith: while she didn't abstain from all indulgences, she mostly preferred healthy eating, like I did.

Faith and I were on the same page about proper nutrition. It made it easy to choose foods wisely and only occasionally indulge in less nutritious options, particularly wine and chocolate—we loved wine and chocolate. But Faith was more obsessive about fitness, especially as she was required to taste fattening foods at the restaurants she was helping. She suffered more guilt after partaking in empty calories than I did. I was more likely to forgive my indiscretions, figuring life was for enjoying, not depriving. But we both felt so much better when we didn't pig out. Staying fit enhanced sex. That was our incentive, and Faith helped keep me on track.

I was just about to place the floral arrangement at the center of the table when I noticed a small gold box. It was imbedded between chocolate-covered grapes and held by a wooden stick with a pineapple daisy on top. Totally stunned, I simply beamed that not only had Faith not forgotten our anniversary but she had bought me a real gift.

"What's this?" I lifted the box, glancing at her for approval like a little girl awaiting permission to open a birthday present, and then ripped open the shiny giftwrap; the tiny bow and paper didn't stand a chance. I lifted the black velvet lid, my hand literally shaking, to find an exquisite solitaire diamond necklace that took my breath away.

"I'm touched beyond belief." Tears leaked out from the corners of my eyes and my voice registered at barely a murmur. "I had no idea."

The timer went off, breaking the spell, but not spoiling the moment. With an oven-gloved hand and dishtowel, I removed the piping hot cast-iron roaster. My whole salmon appeared as if swimming in a sea of fragrant juices amongst tiny bubbles. Steam quickly heated my cheeks, which were already pink with pleasure. I placed the scalding dish on top of the stove while Faith closed the clasp of the necklace. Without checking the salmon for doneness, I scurried to the bathroom mirror to see how I looked. Faith eventually came up and stood behind me as I fingered the jewel that reminded me of an engagement ring, only better.

"Selecting the diamond was easy, but I wasn't sure what length chain would be best. This fits you perfectly."

"Oh Faith, I love you so much. This is the nicest surprise ever. It's exquisite. Thank you." After words failed to express my true emotions, I stopped rambling and planted tons of kisses onto her, painting her lips and face with my love instead.

"Happy anniversary, beautiful." Faith managed a murmur during the rare moment when her mouth was free. "You're smothering me."

"Sorry."

"No, I like it, but we should probably eat before dinner gets cold." She led me by the hand back to the kitchen, where I lit the candles and she popped opened the champagne. "To us," we toasted.

"You've outdone yourself, Janalyn. I rate this meal five out of five stars. But now I'm pleasantly stuffed. I can't eat another bite." Faith pushed her chair away from the table and stood. "I think I'll take my shower now unless you need me to help clean up."

"The dishes can wait. I'd rather help with your shower." I smiled brightly.

Again, Faith led the way, and I was eager to follow. In the bathroom, I stripped her clothes off first. Cool air, in contrast to my warm, wet kisses, constricted her nipples to fine points. Mine tightened in response. It seemed she could hardly contain her desire; nor could I. With haste, she removed my dress, gasping at discovering I had nothing on underneath.

"Oh my, my." Her eyes darkened. Both of us vibrating with unmistakable need, we stepped into the shower, now hot and steamy. I soaped up her slick body, rinsing her off using the handheld showerhead, and when we were done, we towel-dried each other off. My body ached for me to get Faith into bed as quickly as possible.

"God, Janalyn. Had I known you were naked under that dress all during dinner, I'd have skipped the food."

Her words were music to my ears. I loved being a tease for her, especially when she responded like this.

"Don't move a muscle." She leaped out of bed, naked.

"Where are you going?" I asked

"Downstairs. Stay put."

"Don't take all day."

Faith reappeared with her incredible edible bouquet. "Time for dessert!"

She fed me chocolate-covered fruit in bed in exchange for having sex in every position imaginable.

At one point, we got out of bed, so that she could fuck me with a strap-on that delivered both anal and vaginal pleasure simultaneously, and I had to stand on tiptoes for prolonged periods of time in order to climax; I swore my thigh muscles were close to snapping. Had I remained in that position another second, I surely would have needed emergency services. When my orgasm exploded, I came so hard that Faith caught me just before I fell in a fine puddle of contented flesh and bone.

Blissful hours passed before we fell asleep in each other's arms, totally sated and exhausted. It was an anniversary to remember.

Saturday morning, I woke refreshed, yet stiff. I stretched awakened muscles I hadn't even known existed. After the crazy, heat of passion positions in which we had found ourselves last night, it's a wonder I could move at all. Our bodies were entwined, our flesh sticky with the enticing aroma of post-sex afterglow. Faith was one minute in dreamy slumber and the next sleepily nibbling on my earlobe, her heated breath tickling me. It was like being on a slow simmer, after so many hours of scalding hot carnal pursuits.

I could luxuriate in the contours of her body for hours and never tire of tasting every inch of her. Her nibbling led to her kissing her way down my neck until I wanted more, much more. I was ready to be taken, to be ravished by her, but our tender moment was rudely interrupted when her cell phone rang at the highest volume.

I have a love-hate relationship with cell phones—one minute wondering how I ever lived without one and the next wanting to flush it down the toilet. There was nothing worse than an annoying ringtone that didn't stop.

"Aren't you going to answer it?" I asked, wincing as I stretched.

She glanced at the screen and swiped *decline*.

"Who would call this early on a Saturday morning?" My bare breasts brushed hers as I reached for the phone, but she moved it out of my reach, so I sat up instead, with my back against the headboard. "Let me speak to them."

"It's work."

"So why didn't you just pick up?" Feeling a sudden chill, I pulled the sheet so it lay just below my chin and rested my cheek on my knees to face her.

"I wanted to discuss it with you before I made a decision."

"What decision?" Why was she waffling? "What do they want?" The tone of my voice rose despite my best efforts to remain calm.

"I know it's our anniversary, but—"

"Oh no, but what?" I pouted.

"But Longhorn Bill's Grill has been slapped with a hefty fine, with a deadline to clean up or pack it in. They want me to fly to Dallas tonight. Oh, Janalyn, I'm so sorry. I won't go if you don't want me to, but the promotion is within reach, and if I don't jump on this, they'll give it to someone else. And well, we all know who would just gloat in my face."

"I know, I know." I swallowed my disappointment. "You go, and when you get back, we'll continue right where we left off. Call them back." I got out of bed and headed to the shower.

I heard Faith say, "I'll catch the next flight and meet you there..." before I closed the door behind me. A hot shower or a cold shower? Either way, I was doomed. A cold shower to quell the longings in my loins, or a hot shower to steam away the loneliness that settled in my gut? And Faith hadn't even left yet.

That night, Faith rang and gushed about my delicious dinner and our intense coupling. I couldn't stop thanking her for the diamond necklace and telling her how much I missed her.

"How's it going over there, though?" I asked. She was a restaurant whisperer. She managed to save more establishments from going under than all the men on her team. I was so damn proud of her and didn't blame her for wanting to shine in a field where women were just being recognized as knowing a thing or two.

"I think they're willing to work within my plan, starting with getting rid of the head chef." Enthusiasm filled her voice. "That was the hardest part too, as the chef is Bill's—the owner's—brother-in-law, and Bill's wife owns half the business. With this and a few other major changes, I believe they have a strong chance of staying viable. What a mess, though. Thank you for understanding." Faith sounded upbeat and completely in her element. This pleased me.

"I'll be waiting for you, so please hurry home and stay safe."

She blew me kisses, and I saved them all. I spent Sunday morning fixing the toilet, planning to surprise Faith with my plumbing prowess. Then I went for a mid-morning run. After my second shower that morning, I was high on endorphins and texted my trusted friend and colleague Debs, on the off chance she was free for a matinee and dinner, nothing fancy, She was, and so we made a plan.

While I lived on Long Island, my best friend, Deborah Foster-Baker, a.k.a. Debs, resided in Manhattan. We often hung out near Roosevelt Field Mall as a suitable midpoint location with lots of options for activities. Driving to meet her took about thirty to forty minutes by car, depending on the Northern State or Long Island Expressway traffic. Her train ride from Penn to Westbury or Carle Place was around the same.

I had wanted to see *The Dark Knight* with Christian Bale and Heath Ledger for some time. Debs was a real pal, not only meeting at the spur of the moment, but agreeing to the movie of my choice. Whenever Faith refused to see another super-hero or sci-fi flick, Debs was my best bet for companionship. Even when our entertainment tastes didn't match, Debs was open to experiencing every genre imaginable. If I wanted to see a movie on the big screen before it went to DVD or cable TV and Faith had no intentions of enduring something she didn't find intellectually gratifying, then she had no objections about me going with a friend. Besides, with Faith often traveling to further locales and wherever demand for her services were required, I think she felt relieved whenever I had plans, perhaps because she felt it absolved her from being away from home so much.

With time to spare, I left the house for the Westbury train station to pick up Debs. As it turned out, I got there a few minutes ahead of time, so I bought us some Dunkin' Donuts coffee.

Debs arrived at the rendezvous point nearest the ticket office of the station just as I pulled up. Her medium-length layered hair, a deep brown with golden highlights and delicate bangs, had long, finger-like locks that pointed to the notable contours of her cheekbones. The way the hairstyle was so freshly coiffed, it nicely framed her oval face.

"Hi there!" I said, as she breezed into my car with a smile. Think Lara Croft from *Tomb Raider* meets *Sex in the City,* and Debs came to mind: athletic, beautiful, savvy, and on any given day, probably hornier than even me. Shocking, but true. She was also a fashion maven, dressing corporate perfect at work and super-sexy at play. She knew what to wear for any occasion and looked hot in everything. She loved shopping at Roosevelt Field.

"This is a nice surprise. You saved me from doing laundry in the dregs of my apartment building." When Debs spoke, she had your undivided attention, because you couldn't look anywhere else but into her dark brown eyes or at her red lips.

"Whew, wouldn't want to waste time off doing mundane chores." I handed her the bag. "Here, I bought you a coffee if you want one."

"Bless you. I didn't have time to drink anything before boarding, but this is just perfect. Thanks."

She took a sip of the brew, light, without sugar and no longer scalding, and replaced the lid. "What happened to your romantic weekend? Faith off on business again?"

"Yes, you guessed it. The anniversary dinner was exceptional, though." I didn't share the details, but I opened my jacket and showed her the diamond instead.

"Oh, wow! This is incredible. *Somebody* put out a lot to deserve it."

"Shut up."

Debs giggled. I pulled away from the curb, and when I didn't elaborate, Debs kindly let the subject drop. Debs and I were close, but that didn't include sharing intimate details about our sex lives. At least I preferred to keep some things private, Debs not so much; but that was her prerogative.

We both loved the film: all two hours and fifty-some-odd minutes of it went by in a flash, and we decided to finish off the night sharing a meal at TGI Friday's.

"No mentioning work, okay?" I said as we walked into the restaurant. It was already crowded, but the wait for a table was tolerable, so we put our name down on the list.

"I'll do you one better. The first one to say anything work-related buys. Deal?"

"Deal," I said, although it was not an easy task after we'd spent years working together within the same department. We had even followed each other up the corporate ladder, where we grew along with an ever-expanding company. Not talking shop was like having a brand-new puppy and not bragging about him or her to anyone who'd listen.

Working together in a business we both believed in went a long way to keeping our dedication and job satisfaction fairly high. It wasn't as if there were never any grievances at all, but as far as jobs went, Scott Spencer Enterprises was more than decent: to motivate us toward healthy lifestyle choices, we received company-subsidized gym memberships, and once we got holiday food vouchers for a thirty-day supply of fresh fruits, salads, and vegetables from a local Korean market. Faith and I saved a fortune that month on our shopping bill.

Debs and I each ordered salad with chargrilled chicken breasts—dressing on the side, minus cheese, bacon and croutons—as our main entrées. We knew the bar-restaurant chain specialized in affordable food and huge portions, a reason it was always busy and, for us, a reason to avoid eating there. But it was near the movie theater, and we had opted for convenience. Still, when our orders arrived, we gaped at the enormity of the portion size.

"This could very well feed a small nation," I quipped.

Debs nodded. They got the order wrong. She started picking out the fattening stuff, but soon gave up.

I tried to catch the waitress's attention, but she was too busy to stop. My stomach was already growling after watching the almost three-hour epic movie without so much as a kernel of popcorn.

"Oh, go for it," Debs said. "You raised your metabolism running this morning, didn't you?"

"That's not the point. How hard is it to get our orders right?"

"At least the dressing is on the side." Debs popped a chunk of chicken into her mouth. "Yummy, but this doesn't taste low fat to me."

"Me neither," I said. "They probably pump the chicken breasts full of saturated fat and salt to make it grill up nicely. It tastes good, but it's not as healthy as it could be."

"Let's not harp and just enjoy," she said, but I couldn't let it go.

"I hate it when I order the healthiest option on the menu and get the exact opposite," I said, but couldn't stop myself from stuffing forkfuls of chicken loaded with bacon and cheddar into my mouth.

While the servers seemed to have been abducted by aliens, the bar staff had plenty of time to talk us into specialty drinks.

"Let's order strawberry daiquiris and really go to hell with ourselves," Debs said.

"You're a very bad influence. I'm driving, so I'll have a taste of your daiquiri, and we can share dessert."

We were much too absorbed in talking about the movie to pick out the bacon and cheese. Debs's drink was to die for, and we shared the Brownie Obsession.

After we'd done all but lick the plate, I put down my spoon and groaned. "I ate way too much."

"Me too. We'll be better tomorrow." Debs had a quick look at her cell phone. "Oh well, it's been real. Let's get the check."

"I guess we split it, since no mention of work was made."

"Imagine that! Where is our waitress anyhow? I need to head home."

"You can crash in our spare room if you want."

"I'm wide awake now. Hopefully, the train will lull me into sleep mode by the time I get back to my apartment. Besides, I don't have any work clothes with me, and the thought of leaving extra early in the morning to grab something just doesn't appeal. But thanks anyway."

I dropped her at the Westbury train station and waited the fifteen minutes for the next train to arrive. We said our goodbyes.

Catching up with Debs was always fun, especially on days off. It took the edge off missing Faith.

Chapter 2

MONDAY MORNING ROLLED AROUND BEFORE I was ready to relinquish my dream: Faith and I were basking on a white sandy beach, sipping mai tais while warm salt water tickled our toes. A warning signal blared in the distance. Serenity vanished before we could react. No raft, we were totally unprepared. But we had each other to cling to.

Just as a huge wave was about to land on our heads, the sound of the alarm clock catapulted me into reality. It was as if someone had thrown a bucket of ice water over my head. With a pounding heart, I hit the clock radio button, hoping I pressed *off* and not *snooze*. As a backup, I had set both my clock and phone alarms. But waking up to music didn't work. If anything, songs or mindless chatter between DJs lulled me back to la-la land. Faith was a much better wake-up call.

Having a low tolerance for toxic substances of any kind, even sugar, I was still feeling sick. I really could have done without TGI Fridays. Even sharing a Brownie Obsession, with enough fat and calories for a whole day, had pushed me way over my limit. I had such trouble sleeping afterwards, made harder because I didn't relish sleeping alone. With a wicked sugar hangover, it was no surprise that the first hour at work on a hectic Monday morning was going to be a total waste, spent removing the cobwebs from my brain and detoxing from eating too much.

By the time I arrived at work, Debs was at her desk, and the office was all abuzz with activity.

"You're early. Show off," I told her.

"Move to Manhattan," she replied.

"And pay through the nose? That's not going to happen."

I grabbed a fistful of memos. Some things at Scott Spencer Enterprises had remained antiquated, like still receiving memos on top of e-mails. "What have we got?"

"You'll see."

The stack of stuff in my hand and on my desk was daunting. Most of our clients were large firms who could well afford to seek out-of-network consulting services and therefore felt they had the right to exacting standards that kept us busy. Scott Spencer Enterprises had a reputation of putting cost-effective programs in place without bankrupting companies before those companies could reap the benefits of improved employee morale and performance. If people were happy and healthy, they were often more productive. It helped to have personal incentives, reward systems and peer support.

I had just turned on my desktop when a dozen pings signaled alerts. Gearing up to get started, the stupid hard drive needed to be rebooted to install updates. This called for multiple caffeine infusions—the Folgers instant at breakfast wasn't cutting it. Why couldn't Mondays start off restful and calm, to ease us back gently into the work week? No, there had to be meetings, memos, computer glitches, and unanticipated extra work piled on—all marked *urgent*. One such message provided a sign-up sheet asking for volunteers to test out a pilot program for motivating staff to move more while still maintaining optimal work performance in sedentary jobs; as if 'voluntary' was in Scott Spencer's son Marcus's vocabulary—which it wasn't.

Naturally, Debs and I were the first names on the list. She made sure of it. Debs worked so hard, but being competent was second nature for her. That's why she volunteered to go the extra mile, so she wouldn't be idle for even a second, and because she was too nosy not to have a finger in every pot, including after-work events. She was always reaching for the stars, an avid overachiever—goal-oriented, perfectionist, yet completely laid back about her achievements; but heaven help anyone she cared about if they didn't tag along.

My cellphone bleeped. It was a text from Faith. I immediately cheered up, reading what she wrote:

How's the sexiest woman alive this morning Xx?

Pining for the object of her fondest desires. You? XXX

Me too. Looking forward to unlimited repeats of the other night's performance.

My thumbs raced through the motions of creating what I hoped looked like us eating each other out.

As usual, work got in the way of real life. The galleys of my handouts arrived ready for the final proofread before they went to print. Seconds later, a box of bound booklets I'd completed the week before landed on my desk with a thud. I had enough to keep me busy for a week, but only two days to do it.

Oops. Gotta run. Have a great day, darling. Love you.

XXX Love you too. Miss you. XXX

I silenced my cell phone and forced myself to ignore kinky images so I could accomplish something constructive that also paid the bills. I finally got back into the groove, losing all track of time and space. After both handouts met my standards, I switched gears completely and dove into a tedious amount of statistical data to analyze—a task that was as much fun as a bout of stomach flu. I couldn't remember how I became the go-to girl for restoring order to records that were a total mess, as if I were the only one who could organize it sensibly. It took hours arranging years of statistics that should have been collected and entered onto the database regularly. I experimented with several approaches to organizing the random facts and figures—chronological, subject, quantity, and success versus failure—all in an attempt to figure out which model would most usefully visualize the improvements I needed to present in my five-year projections. Focusing on the computer screen too long made my eyeballs burn, but I was completely absorbed.

When the gentle tapping of Debs's knuckle on my desk made me jump, I was glad it was her, but I still blurted out, "Geez, Debs, use a sledgehammer, why don'tcha."

"*Someone* is grouchy."

"They fire Todd and leave me with his shit to clean up. You'd be grouchy too."

"Poor baby. But we're talking Christmas, which is sooner than you think, so priorities, my dear friend; this is important. We're having the holiday party at the VFW Hall this year."

I pounded my keyboard. "This stupid program is getting on my nerves—it keeps freezing up at the worst possible moment."

"You're not listening."

I glanced up at her, briefly. "FYI, Miss Party Pants, I *was* paying close attention."

"Close attention, hrmpff. Well, Miss Attentive, what did I say, and, more importantly, what do you think?"

I closed the program with a huff and pushed my chair as far away from the cluttered desk as it would go, which was not very far at all. Even a tiny distance between me and my work for a much-needed break was better than fighting with a finicky computer that screamed, *we need a newer model here, ASAP.*

The muscles around my mouth slackened, and a tiny hint of a smile started.

"I think that following up last year's five-star Christmas party at that fancy-schmancy Continental restaurant—which ended up being fun and festive beyond everyone's expectations—with a Christmas party at the VFW is, well, cheesy," I said.

"Well, Janalyn Jacobs, why don't you tell us how you really feel?"

"I'm just being a realist."

"But you don't have to be so negative, and you are allowed to breathe, even during tirades. What you need is more coffee to lift your spirits."

She held out her hand. I spun my chair around and passed her my mug as she breezed by. We took turns supporting each other's caffeine habit.

Without missing a beat, Debs walked the few steps across the office to the communal pantry that housed the various amenities of a studio apartment kitchen, including a small gas stove for members of staff who preferred to prepare their lunches at the office rather than go out to eat. I caught a whiff of freshly brewed coffee, could tell it was strong, and got an instant buzz before even taking the first sip.

Debs handed me my mug and warmed both her hands on hers. "Oh God, don't look now, but the administrative assistant's secretary, what's her name, is at it again."

I moved everything to one side so we could have our coffee break together. She then wheeled her chair to my side of the partition.

"What's she done now?"

"Can't you smell it? She's obviously vying for a promotion," Debs said.

I sniffed the air, and sure enough, I could detect cookie dough baking, namely three scrumptious varieties. "Yum, if I had to guess, she's making chocolate chip, white chocolate macadamia nut and peanut butter cookies. Do I win?"

"Ding, ding, ding. Right you are. How do you correctly identify three varieties of cookies?"

"It's a talent." I sat up taller. "And I have a bionic nose, inherited from my mother, who could tell who ate what from her kitchen just from sniffing our breaths." I laughed. "There never was any getting away with swiping some goodies when she wasn't looking. Besides all that, I saw a bag of macadamia nuts on her desk the other day, and I could identify chocolate chip and peanut butter in a snap."

Debs swatted my arm. "That's cheating. I'd say..." She wiggled my mouse to get the time from the desktop, "...in about seven minutes, thirty one seconds, I will go over there and confiscate some for us."

"Swell idea. Only, it's Monday, we ate like pigs last night, and I'm trying to be good."

"Oh pooh, forget diets. Faith has you so tightly strung when it comes to food, if you ask me. Besides, you're already perfect. Look at you: there's not an ounce of unwanted fat or flesh anywhere."

"Dark clothes can be deceiving."

"Nonsense. I've seen you naked, and I know exactly what I'm talking about. You have an amazing body, a flat stomach, tits that don't sag, and perfectly sculpted legs most women would give up their most prized possessions for. You have no idea how many wet dreams have dried up when the guys I know find out you're a lesbian. You have no freaking idea what a heartbreaker you are!"

If Debs wasn't as straight as an unwinding road, her compliment would make me blush from here to kingdom come, but alas, changing in the locker room at the YMCA after heavy aerobics followed by swimming laps for an hour hardly counted as seeing each other naked in a sexual way. It was a good thing I didn't get to ponder her comment for too long, for although my face was growing hot, Debs was already on to other subjects.

"I hear she prepares the dough at home. From scratch! I have no clue where she finds the time to work, bake and put on enough makeup for a show on Broadway. She's in before we are, and have you ever seen her leave on time? What gives?"

Relieved to steer the conversation away from my so-called finer attributes, I played the gossip game instead, although it wasn't my favorite pastime. My feelings for Debs, who by the way was a total babe, were deep-seated and totally platonic, since I had Faith. To a fault, I was faithful. The pun made me laugh.

Back to contemplating the secretary with the obvious implants in both her breasts and butt. "I think Amber's either a gold digger or she has the hots for Mr. Nerdly." The image of Miss Playboy Centerfold and her boss as a couple got us both laughing. Syd was the biggest nerd in NYC, hands down. He brought new meaning to socially inept—emotionally befuddled yet mentally brilliant—an all-around geek who never ceased to find new ways to torment us all. If he wasn't such a slave driver, we could really appreciate his smarts.

It wasn't long before the office smelled as mouthwatering as a bakery. I had no idea how Faith resisted when she worked around kitchens all day long, sometimes seven days a week. I tried to channel her fortitude, but it took heroic strength to suppress the delightful salivary response to such heavenly aroma.

"For a company that promotes health and well-being, how the heck does anyone get away with tempting each other with tasty empty-calorie treats? That's what I want to know," I said.

"Beats me. But we can afford it."

"Says who? Usually there are enough chocolates, cakes, cookies and pastries around here to pad the waistlines and hips of every already bulging body. Never mind that most of us are trying to watch our weight and promote positive lifestyle habits." I patted my belly to check that it wasn't going completely to pot. "It's our company mission to make healthy choices; but that's near impossible around here."

"Okay, Miss Preacher, you can step down from your soapbox now. You're singing to the choir. I agree with you. We have to set a fine example, no matter how hard that may be. Move more, eat less—that's our motto. Oh, and my all-time favorite, have tons and tons of calorie-burning sex," Debs said.

I laughed. "I really don't think senior Spencer, or even junior, have sex in the recipe for weight loss success."

"Probably not. Come with me to the gym after work so we can eat these cookies and get away with it."

"I don't have my stuff."

"We can buy something on the way or stop at my place. You can borrow mine."

"I'll think about it," I said. Debs had a convincing argument for every scenario. Of course I would join her at the gym. How could I not?

I heard the egg timer ring, and without spending another second thinking about waistlines, calories, or anything but sinking my teeth into gooey chewy, chocolate chip cookies right out of the oven, I told Debs with gusto, "Go get 'em, cowgirl."

"That's the spirit!" Debs hurried over, joining the stampede.

"Oh my God, won't she miss all those?" She had a plate heaping with cookies when she returned to my desk.

"Are you kidding? There's enough for every department plus leftovers. Dig in."

With our coworker Patrick, the senior member of the team and self-appointed know-it-all, off for the day, we continued to chat, taking a longer than usual but much-needed break, as Debs filled our mugs a second time, adding sugar and Cremora Lite to hers and leaving mine black. Give me the real thing or don't give me anything. That was *my* motto, not that I didn't appreciate Debs's idea of having copious amounts of sex for exercise.

"*Anyway*," Debs said, "the VFW Hall was Patrick's idea." She clearly still hadn't gotten over my remarks about her work party proposal. "He says the money we'll save on a less fancy venue can be spent on live entertainment. We'll even have extra cash for good food from a reputable caterer of my choosing." Debs smiled broadly. She so loved being in charge. And it really was her forte.

"No way is he going to let anyone else choose the menu and entertainment."

"It's true. Patrick claims he's a food and wine connoisseur, and it's evident he has the girth to match, so I'll allow him the final say on the food. But the entertainment—"

"Whose idea was it to have us dress up as elves and reindeer last year, so that our secret Santa couldn't tell us apart to hand out the right gift to the right person?"

"You have to admit, we made a pretty mean pack of elves," she said.

I couldn't help but join her snicker. "There's no such thing as tall, mean elves that run in packs. The ones I imagine are all short and sweet."

"You're much too technical. Anyways, Pat isn't in charge of the entertainment—I am." Debs buffed her nails on the lapel of her navy pinstriped suit.

"Do tell how you managed that one." My ears perked up. I suddenly had a good feeling about this.

"I've booked the Azteks."

"No way!" They were probably the hottest local club band around, with Latin beats and plenty of salsa. "They must charge a fortune."

"They do, but I'm dating the lead singer's brother, and, well, let's just say I got us a really good deal."

"You never cease to amaze me. Wait until I tell Faith; she'll flip. The Azteks are her latest craze. We can bring a date, right? Faith will love me for bringing her along."

"Of course you can, but it'll cost you. We have to keep to a budget. I figure that for the price of a top-notch band and food ordered from Five Star Caterers, nobody will make too much noise about paying for a date when they're getting their evening for free."

"You're a genius, Debs."

As we did often, we reached to wiggle the mouse out of screen-saver mode, glanced at the desktop and gasped. The long coffee break ended up counting as our lunch hour.

I went back to making sense of Excel and by the end of the day had a working copy of projections to be revised ad nauseam, and Debs decided that she was satisfied with her latest project.

I was almost ready to call it a day when my cell phone made noise, and I picked it up on the first ring, after almost deciding to let it go to voicemail. My face lit up when I heard Faith's voice.

"Hi, beautiful. How's my girl?"

"Wonderful, now that I'm speaking to you."

"Good. I'm running a bit late and won't be home before eleven at the earliest. I had to catch the later flight. Sorry to miss dinner, but you can have the leftovers if you want."

"No problem. I might hit the gym, then and have a salad when I get home." I was still full from too many cookies and buzzed from downing copious amounts of coffee.

"That's a great idea. Wish I could join you. I could use a good workout, followed by further toning."

I knew what she meant by toning. We were both in longstanding agreement that sex was great for developing muscles other exercises missed.

"I love you," I whispered into the mouthpiece. The office staff had thinned considerably, but there were still plenty of peeps who would love nothing better than have something to wag their tongues about.

"Love you too. Have a great workout."

I knocked on Debs's cubicle. "Looks like I'm definitely gymming with you tonight. I need a new swimsuit. Can I borrow those extra goggles and towel?"

"Of course; be ready in a sec."

On the way to the Y, I picked up a Speedo swimsuit, Lycra capris because they were greatly reduced, a package of cushioned sport socks (always handy), and a cheap nondescript T-shirt. When we entered the locker room at the gym, I had an unexpected case of nerves about changing in front of Debs after her earlier comment about seeing me naked. But thoughts of keeping in tip-top shape for Faith soon dispelled any anxiety. Besides, Debs opted for the treadmill, StairMaster and weights, while I headed straight into the pool. The swim did wonders for not missing Faith too much until she got home. Afterward, I bid Debs goodnight.

I was completely stoked that Faith was coming home. It didn't matter how late—I'd wait up just to kiss her goodnight. The trip from Penn to the Ronkonkoma station and then our front door happened in a flash when my mind was preoccupied imagining lust-filled reunions. As much as I hated her being away all the time, all these business trips sure did keep the heart growing ever fonder. Faith and I never seemed to get a chance to get sick of each other.

Faith came home late Monday night, as promised. Actually, she tiptoed in at three a.m., technically Tuesday morning. I barely remembered kissing her in my drowsy state, but I do remember being spooned back to sleep. The next morning, at breakfast, there was no mention of Faith rushing off again soon, and I was content that we could enjoy our evenings together and plan for the upcoming weekend.

The week really flew once the routine was restored. At the office, Debs and I were totally engrossed in work: the test pilot program was in full swing, which meant taking the stairs instead of elevators, walking around the office every hour, standing and stretching at our desks, and engaging in light calisthenics. At first, everyone laughed their heads off when they weren't too busy grumbling about wasting precious time, but soon, the bell would ring throughout the office, and like well-trained dogs, we did as told without a peep. It seemed that the volunteer sheet was just a ploy, because every single person on our floor was involved. In between light exercising, we attended short films and pep talks on proper nutrition and the benefits of even moderate physical activity—all the stuff Debs and I knew by heart, but had to listen to regardless. We were encouraged to leave work at a reasonable time, even if that time was often a few hours after our shifts ended, and to hit the pavement for a power walk or the gym of our choice at least five out of seven days a week.

Debs and I had no problem with this. After being chocolated-out by Monday's stash of cookies, we had successfully avoided office goodies altogether, hoping the admin secretary took the hint and stopped baking. But by Thursday, she showed no sign of letting up, and we gave in, sneaking one cookie each, so as not to alert anyone we weren't giving one hundred percent. Besides, neither of us felt we needed to be perfect in order to be healthy. We high-fived to moderation as we nibbled at our indiscretion in the supply room when no one was looking. Only a handful of coworkers fell off the wagon, more than once, and some stayed off. I figured non-compliance into the success rate percentages—it was inevitable.

By the time I left work on Friday, stopped for a session at the gym, and then headed for home, I was floating on air, already planning extra cuddle time with Faith. Debs had finalized the Azteks and left a huge non-refundable deposit, and I had impulsively bought tickets that day for both me and Faith before leaving work, even though I hadn't asked Faith about it yet. I wanted to surprise her with the tickets over dinner one night soon. I could already imagine the excitement on her face when I told her. Sure, it was a bit risky to buy the tickets before asking, but surely, work wouldn't send Faith anywhere over Christmas or New Year's; what restaurant would want someone poking her nose into their set routines during one of the biggest customer spending seasons?

Yes, I was certain it was a done deal. Even if work tried to schedule her, Faith would get out of any obligation to see the Azteks; I was sure of it.

I pulled the Mazda into the driveway beside Faith's Camry, surprised she had beaten me home. I glanced at my watch, verifying that she was an hour earlier than usual and grabbed my briefcase off the floor by the passenger seat. Followed by the seventy-five laps Debs and I had done in forty-nine minutes, seeing Faith home waiting for me for a change had me on endorphin overload.

The gravel under my rubber soles had a nice feel to it. Maybe we shouldn't pave the driveway after all, I thought. I juggled my work stuff along with my new purchases and a Ziploc baggie filled with the leftover cookies Debs insisted I take, because Playboy Bunny had gone rabid, and the result was non-stop baking. At Debs's suggestion, I planned to hide the cookies in the freezer as an emergency stash for when the test pilot ended and Faith was not on the lookout. I prepared myself for a battle of lock and key when the front door swung open the minute I arrived at the top step.

Faith held a briefcase and an overnight bag in each hand. Her handbag was slung across her chest. Every hair was in place. She smelled nice too.

"Where are you going?" I asked.

"Oh Janalyn, I left you a note. Something happened, and I'm flying into BWI tonight."

"No! Where are you flying to?"

"A new client with an upscale restaurant in Georgetown. I'm not even at liberty to reveal the name of the establishment. This is a huge make-or-break deal; I can't afford to miss this one."

I dreaded another weekend alone. "For how long this time?"

"One or two days, tops; maybe three. I'll call as soon as I know the details."

"But you only just got home Monday, and it's the weekend." I looked down at my feet, vacillating between exploding with anger and bursting into tears.

"I know." At least she had the decency to look positively despondent. "Come here, you."

I dropped my stuff on the floor by our feet and fell into her arms. She smelled absolutely gorgeous. I could have wept. I mumbled into her neck. "It's almost Christmas. I thought we'd go shopping, buy new outfits, gifts and—"

"You don't have to remind me, but you know what it's like. I'm close to this promotion, so close I can't blow it."

"Please, cancel your trip. Don't go." Sounding more like a crybaby by the second, I did my best not to whine; it wasn't working. "Please conference call or e-mail or whatever you can. I'll give you plenty of space to work from home. *Please.*"

"You know I need to see for myself before I assess the situation. Besides, I can hardly sample their menu online. You know that, Janalyn. I'll miss my flight."

"I'll take you to the airport."

"I've already prepaid the parking at the airport. This way, you won't have to worry if I get back early or late."

"Debs booked The Azteks for the holiday party this year. Please promise you're not working through Christmas too."

Faith stopped dead for a split second, the wild look of excitement about the prospects of spending the night dancing to salsa performed by none other than Manhattan's own, obviously gave her something to contemplate. But as quickly as I caught the fervent excitement of a true fan in her eyes, it was gone: she pursed her lips and shook her head.

"No? Please tell me you can take one night off." Disappointment solidified into anger. "The party's two weeks away. Surely you can switch with someone."

"Janalyn, please. Don't make this harder than it has to be. You'll make me late. We'll discuss it when I get back. Now give me a kiss, and I'm off."

With nothing more I could say or do to persuade her to forgo this assignment, I simply went back into the house and closed the old oak door without even watching her leave. She was right: the promotion would be great for her and would help us with all the repairs and bills; our costs in this area were indeed formidable. I'd lived in an apartment for so long before buying my first house, I had no idea what a huge undertaking and money pit an old vintage house like this would turn out to be.

I looked around the house we called home. Sometimes I envied Debs and her recently updated digs; all she had to do was freshen up the paint and redecorate. Faith and I had already upgraded the electrical system, repaired the heating several times, and put in a new hot water heater, after we'd realized we couldn't flush the toilet, run the sink, and take a shower at the same time. In fact, after doing a load of laundry in warm water, forget about running a bath or using hot water at all, because not only did it waste electricity, we also had to wait at least thirty minutes for the water to heat up again. What in the beginning had been a romantic, rustic home had soon turned into something chronically annoying.

Faith was right to work hard. She was always right. Who was I to complain when all she wanted was to make our lives easier? I fingered the anniversary present around my neck and felt a pang of guilt. I loved her so much, it hurt to be apart, but I would be okay. There was plenty for me to concentrate on here. Maybe it was as good a chance as any to catch up on work from home. At least we had the latest computer equipment at home; Faith's overtime certainly helped on that account.

Suddenly, I couldn't wait for her to arrive wherever she was headed, so I could call and make it up to her.

Chapter 3

AFTER FAITH GOT HOME FROM Georgetown, she didn't mention any other trips on the horizon, but she was unusually quiet during dinner. She barely touched the crustless quiche I had whipped up with the odds and ends left in the fridge. And I could hear myself chew and swallow; I hated that.

I finished another forkful of quiche and bit the end of the sweet potato, skin and all. Washing it down with a gulp of seltzer, I hiccupped. Faith usually laughed when carbonation made me hiccup, saying something silly like, "Need drinking lessons?" to which I sometimes sang, "How dry I am..." But this time, the silence between us was deafening.

Unable to believe I even had to ask, I finally did anyway: "What's the matter?"

"Nothing, just tired."

It wasn't like her to be moody. I patted the top of her hand. "When was the last time you had a full check-up?" She didn't turn up her palm so we could intertwine our fingers as usual.

"I have regular check-ups; you know that. I'm just tired, so can we give it a rest?" She had just made a pun, and she didn't even smile about it. She just stood and took her plate over to the garbage can, dumping untouched food.

"Well, that was a waste," I said.

"I'm sorry, I'm not very hungry. I'll be upstairs answering e-mails."

"Fine."

I had done the bulk of the dishes as I had prepared dinner, so there wasn't much left to wash by hand. After the plates, glasses and silverware were stacked on the draining board, I wiped my hands on a dishtowel and busied myself to avoid dwelling on what was going on in Faith's mind. I covered the Pyrex dish of leftover quiche with foil. I could eat it again, but probably wouldn't. I then contemplated packing a lunch for the next day. Absently, I opened the refrigerator, stared inside without seeing a thing, and shut the door.

With no reason left to delay any further, I mounted the staircase. Colonial-style houses were notorious for long and winding staircases, suitable for grand exits and entrances. Imagine running up the stairs at Tara in *Gone with the Wind*. It didn't matter that I wasn't wearing a rib-crushing corset and cumbersome attire that weighed a ton: the heaviness in my chest increased with each step I took, until I felt like I should be gasping as I headed to the guest bedroom, which doubled as a study where Faith was busy right now, answering e-mails.

Her back was to me as I entered the study. Lost in thought, I looked around the room, each side with its own desk, filing cabinet, built-in shelving, and sofa bed.

We never had guests. Faith wasn't even around enough to invite them anyway. While it had never bothered me before, in this moment, it made me furious. My family had only stayed for dinner once in the whole time we had been living here. I resolved right then and there to invite them again soon, with or without Faith.

"What are you working on?" I asked.

Faith quickly closed her e-mail and turned to face me. "Work stuff—nothing too exciting."

"I'll go wash up. Maybe there's a good movie on TV." Not that I could concentrate on anything, but what was the use of dwelling on things beyond my control? I hoped whatever had Faith acting out-of-character would be resolved, the quicker the better.

"I'll be in soon."

It took a lot to get me worked up. It wasn't like Faith had never been in a bad mood before. She'd have her rant and be done with it, problem solved and soon forgotten. But I didn't know what to do with her quiet distress. I internalized endless possibilities of disaster.

This was ridiculous. Shaking my head to clear my mind of wasteful clutter, I prepared a steamy shower; that would calm me.

Faith was in bed reading when I was finished in the shower. I flashed my naked body before her, but her response didn't promise an invitation to play, so I chucked the towel in the hamper and slipped into my PJs. It had been almost a week, and we hadn't had sex; I couldn't stand it a minute longer.

I sat on my side of the bed. She continued to read from a food service journal.

"Is everything all right, Faith?"

"Yes, of course."

"Then why do I get the feeling you're not telling me something?"

"Because you're paranoid," she snapped.

What she said wasn't as harsh as the *way* she said it. I couldn't think of anything I had said or done to deserve this unfair treatment. I doubted it was PMS: Faith had been on the pill since before we met. I thought it was odd for a lesbian to be on oral contraceptives, but Faith claimed the hormones in the pill kept her PMS under control and helped lessen her monthly flow.

"Please just tell me what's on your mind."

She placed the magazine down and scooted over for a hug. "Oh Janalyn, I'm sorry I'm being such a bitch. I really hate this, but—"

"But?"

"I know you want me to come with you to your Christmas party, and you know I love the Azteks, but something did truly come up at work, and I have to go."

I pulled away, feeling the wound all over again. "I had already purchased a ticket for you." Unable to stifle the tremor, I raised my voice. "It wasn't cheap."

"I know, that's why I feel—"

"I don't care how you feel, Faith." The anger rose within me like mercury in a thermometer held under a flame. "I've done the math, and you know what? My calculations tell me that this past month alone, you've put business ahead of us sixty percent of the time. You've been away eighteen days. It's a bit much, don't you think?"

Silence ensued until it made me sick.

"Say something? Is your job really more important to you than I am?"

"No, never. Only—"

"Oh save it. We didn't get to see the foliage or go apple picking. You didn't have Thanksgiving with us, disappointing not just me but my parents too. I'm sick to death of spending holidays, weekends and even weeknights alone. I'm sleeping in the other room."

I stormed out, taking my pillow with me. My mother always said the key to a good relationship was never to go to bed mad, but to hell with that. I deserved to be hurt, angry and disappointed. Who wouldn't?

It was cold in the guest room. Decorative pillows and sofa cushions went flying as I flung them onto the floor, knocking over the wastebasket, spilling crumpled papers. I didn't bother to clean the mess, but instead opened the sofa bed, grumbling at the sight of a bare mattress. Having little energy left in me to make up a bed, I just closed it back up and prepared to sleep on the couch.

Once settled, I pulled the blanket up to my chin and sulked. Never mind that I couldn't get the money back for the ticket, I had told everyone she was going. Even Patrick, our company dinosaur, who I thought would be the biggest homophobe on the planet said he was happy he'd finally get to meet my girlfriend at the Christmas party. I had been looking forward to showing Faith off.

Faith went to great lengths to cheer me up, leaving me little surprises, such as a small notepad with a skinny pen that fit inside a jacket pocket, because I was forever jotting down things I mustn't forget. She left a stuffed puppy holding a heart by my pillow and even bought us tickets to the theater in May, third row center to see *Billy Elliot*. It was impossible to stay mad for long.

Christmas came and went with Faith working as usual, but she tried her best to be home more than she was away. I had helped Debs with a lot of the planning for the work Christmas party, so that helped ease the pain as well. The Azteks were amazing, and we managed to throw one heck of a good company party, if I do say so myself. It was a shame Faith had missed it, but after the fight we'd had, things between us seemed to improve. Whenever she was around, I felt closer to her than ever. My outburst had served as a wake-up call for her, it seemed. It eased my mind, knowing that she would do anything not to lose me, as if she ever could.

Unfortunately, it wasn't long into the new year before Faith's out-of-state assignments stretched out again to longer chunks of time. I couldn't keep track if she was in Dallas, Miami, San Francisco, Chicago, or any other place that wasn't with me where she belonged. I suppose another woman would have suspected Faith might have a little chickie on the side, but I knew better and never doubted Faith for a second.

After another lonely weekend, I went back and forth between wondering if we should consider adopting a puppy. But I still couldn't believe how much I had accomplished during another weekend home alone. Aside from running and a bit of gardening, I stayed in, worked, and cleaned. I didn't even call Debs, not wanting to make her cancel her date just to cheer me up. As long as I kept up a constant pace, I was fine. The moment I stopped to relax, I became restless.

They say April showers bring May flowers, and boy did it rain. But the dreary weather, while good for all I had planted, made it a ton less painful that Faith wasn't there to share the outdoors with me. I ended up ahead of the game on my latest project. I let myself become caught up in work, even with tedious tasks, just to keep my mind off Faith traveling so often. But, feeling lonesome for my lover had its advantages too: my heart certainly grew fonder in Faith's absence, and when we finally had the luxury of spending time together, we sure made the most of it.

But this had to end sometime.

As the Monday mornings I awoke without Faith piled up over time, I began arriving at the office a few minutes early; there was no sense lingering in an empty bed. By ten a.m., the air around my cubicle was hot and stuffy as usual. Scott Spencer rented three floors of office space from absentee landlords who didn't care much about their tenants, only about collecting the obscene rents on time. They either blasted us with heat starting from Thanksgiving or didn't start the air-conditioning until after Memorial Day.

But heat wasn't why I had the top three buttons of my blouse open. Certainly not for the first time, I grabbed my pocket mirror to check the clasp of my new necklace and examine the way it sparkled. Even four months later, it shone as brilliantly as the day Faith clasped it to my neck.

"You're a changed woman, Janalyn," Debs said from her desk.

"How do you mean?"

"You are having an affair with a necklace."

I stuck my tongue out at her. "I am not!" I then turned serious. "This is just a mere trinket, but Faith gave it to me, so it's my duty to protect it as a token of our love."

"Gag me." Debs went back to her computer and typed away about a hundred words a minute.

I ignored her and checked my necklace again. Sure enough, the solitaire diamond was definitely not a figment of my imagination. It was a tangible testament to how much I meant to Faith. She had spent a pretty penny on it, and I was delighted to think that she had gone to such great pains to secretly buy the necklace without me having an inkling until I opened the box.

I'd never owned an expensive piece of jewelry that I cared as much about, not even the chic costume stuff. It was a given that I was never taking the necklace off, and hadn't, not even to swim or bathe. I had hardly expected I'd end up appreciating a diamond as much as I did until I actually owned one. But what really got me about Faith's generous gesture was that her buying habits were too controlled and calculated to happen on a whim. She wasn't cheap, but she was discerning. If my anniversary present wasn't bought haphazardly, then perhaps it meant that Faith and I should consider taking our relationship to the next step.

Thirteen years, four months, and three days and going strong. Maybe I should put a ring on it. The more I imagined the prospect of a formal declaration in a court of law that would recognize our love, the wider my smile.

My work prospectus practically wrote itself. A short time before noon, Debs came by my desk. "You still *game* to give Vegan Plus a chance?"

Vegan Plus was a new upscale vegetarian restaurant nearby that we had decided to check out to see if it was worth recommending to others. I'm not a vegetarian, much less a vegan, but for health reasons, I tried my best to include meatless options often.

"Okeydokey, but 'game' is not vegan."

Debs shook her head trying not to laugh.

"Let me save this doc." I jumped up and slipped on my jacket, glanced out the window at clear blue skies for a change, and left my umbrella behind.

"Let's rock and roll then. I'm starved," Debs said. She shrugged into her suit jacket. Over a cream-colored camisole, it added elegance to the crisp lines of her suit.

"I had no idea I was this hungry either," I said as we walked through Manhattan's lunch hour crowd.

The line to get into the corner restaurant was out the door and around the block.

"I didn't know there were this many vegetarians in Midtown!"

"Nor I. Maybe they're giving it away," I said.

"I doubt it. Thank God I made reservations." Debs rubbed her grumbling belly. We all were missing the presence of Amber, the office Playboy Bunny and baking temptress, who had been transferred to another department after management got wind of her deep infatuation with Syd, which bordered on stalking. Our hungry stomachs were paying the price, even if our hips were thanking us these days.

"I have something to ask you, but at this rate, I'll start digesting my own stomach before I get a chance to talk to you about it." I peered through the glass at the crowded waiting area, wondering if the number of patrons violated some fire code.

"Okay, Miss Drama Queen, leave it to me." Debs walked up to the door and spoke with the man holding the clipboard. Within minutes, she waved me over.

I could tell the man was completely taken with her. It was hard not to be. Even I was still a victim to her charms.

"Would you believe that even with reservations, he wanted us to wait forty-five minutes?" she told me as we took our seats.

"Well then, I guess we're lucky that you turned out to be his type," I teased.

"Luck had nothing to do with it," Debs eyes scanned the menu. "Now, what's on your mind, Janalyn?"

"I need ideas for the perfect marriage proposal."

That pulled her eyes from the menu. "Ahhhhh, you're going for it, good for you." She gave me her undivided attention the moment we placed our orders. Had the shoe been on the other foot, I don't know if I would have been as generous as Debs, knowing her significant other hated me, sight unseen, the way Faith did Debs. It was a real sticking point between me and Faith, but I had stopped sharing details about how Debs and I had done this or that to avoid confrontation on the home front.

Still, Debs was a doll. She listened patiently while I obsessed about making an honest woman of Faith. "I don't care if same-sex marriage isn't legal in New York," I said, "because I'm prepared to tie the knot in any state that'll recognize us."

"Way to go!" I loved how Debs supported me no matter what. Why couldn't Faith be as tolerant of Debs? I should have known it was a bad sign that whenever I made plans for her and Debs to meet, she'd have an unexpected business conflict. Debs forgave all that, and despite never having met Faith, she didn't have an unkind word to say about her. If I loved Faith, then that's all Debs needed to know.

She put her thinking cap on, cracking me up as she tied the imaginary strings, and started to bombard me with feasible scenarios.

"How about you ask her on ice at Rockefeller Center followed by dinner at The Sea Urchin?" Debs suggested.

"Faith has weak ankles, she's likely to break something, and she's allergic to shellfish. Besides, it's nearly May. Doesn't the rink shut down from April until October? I want to do this before she leaves for Dubai in July."

"Dubai? I thought her company stayed on this continent?"

"They're branching out."

"Oh. Okay then, how about booking a helicopter ride overlooking Manhattan?"

"She's afraid of heights."

"That is a problem." But Debs remained undaunted. "I know! You're both from Brooklyn. Propose to her on the Brooklyn Bridge at sunset."

"That sounds romantic, but how do I get her there without raising suspicion?"

"Easy, you tell her you've always wanted to view the sunset over the East River and that walking to the restaurant would be good exercise too. You can have a fancy meal and tons of champagne at a place near the Brooklyn Heights promenade. Very romantic."

"You're a genius! That sounds perfect. Thanks, Debs."

"No problem. Happy to help." Her voice turned sardonic. "Besides, my ex didn't have a romantic bone in his body. Well, maybe one, and even that was iffy. I don't mind living vicariously through you and Faith."

"You're so much better off without him." I still wanted to pulverize the louse she'd married right out of college. From our introduction, I had had a funny feeling about him, and I'd been right: he'd hurt her time and time again before she divorced him.

"I know, but if you hadn't been there to scrape me off the floor, I don't know how I would have coped. What an ordeal divorce is! If I wasn't straight, I'd marry you today."

"Oh Debs, you flatter me way too much; you're the better catch. Your ex-husband was a jerk. Too bad about the Azteks's lead singer's brother too. He was very polite and sure was nice to look at, if you like tall, dark and extremely handsome men."

"He was much too vain for me. Sure, he was a good lay, the best, but I had to wait hours for him to primp. What girl wants to put up with that?"

I laughed.

"Besides, he was the biggest mama's boy. I would not be happy coming in second to his mother, and she hated me the moment we met. I wasn't Latin American, for one, and I wasn't willing to let her dictate our every waking moment. Anyway, even without *la madre* from hell, it would never have worked. He was too pretty for me."

"You're too pretty for him is more like it. Oh well, his loss. As long as you're okay with the split."

"Hell yeah, plenty of other fish to fry, I mean catch."

"Hear, hear." I raised my glass of seltzer, and we toasted to making honest women of ourselves sooner rather than later. I vowed to keep an eye out for the perfect man for her, and she would keep her fingers crossed that my proposal was awesome.

"You will invite me to the wedding?"

"Of course," I said quickly, but I had a nagging feeling that it would be too small a wedding for any guests who weren't doubling as legal witnesses. Debs would be my first choice of witness, but I guessed Faith would insist on her sister, since I could never choose just one of my four brothers. But there was time later to worry about that. I had a proposal idea and all I needed was to work out the details.

Debs scurried off to pay the bill, since vegetarian was her idea. When she returned, I helped her into her jacket.

"Sometimes I wonder if I'll ever meet the right man. Don't get me wrong, I love my life, my job, my apartment, and even my indoor plants are thriving, but it gets lonely, you know."

"Tell me about it."

"Sorry, I know Faith is away too much. Way, way too much."

"No need to apologize, I know what you mean though. I have every confidence that your Prince Charming is out there. Mark my words," I said, with conviction, repeating, "Mark my words."

"Your words to God's ears," she murmured. I said a little prayer myself.

She smiled. "That was really good for being totally animal free."

I nodded. "I give them five stars and bet Faith would give her seal of approval too. Plus, thanks to you, I have a plan for the proposal. Thank you."

We hugged on it and left arm-in-arm. I can't even remember the rest of the afternoon. I was going to ask Faith to be my wife, and I was the happiest woman alive.

Chapter 4

Summer 2008

THE DAY I PLANNED TO take our relationship to the next level had started off with a delightful dawn chorus right outside our bedroom window. Leave it to a well-stocked bird feeder with just the right food to attract the best songbirds. I would have loved to reach over to her side of the bed to plant a morning kiss on Faith's lips, but once again, she wasn't there. Once again, her job had waltzed into our life. But this time it was because Faith had set off earlier than usual to make sure she could leave work in plenty of time to make our dinner date that night. So this absence didn't get me down. Not today.

Eager to start my day, I jumped out of bed. While I brushed my teeth, after removing the whitening strips, I smiled at my reflection. My dazzling white teeth were almost as sparkly as my diamond necklace. I hoped Faith liked the diamond wedding band as much as I had loved my anniversary present.

After months of careful planning and fretting that I'd slip and spoil the surprise, my nerves were shot. Surely I wasn't the first lover to stress about proposing. My concerns were not so much out of fear she'd say no, but more about everything not going smoothly when, for me, only sheer perfection would do.

I stared into the mirror and grinned back at my reflection. Come tomorrow morning, I'd be a new woman. Already, I felt like an old married lady, but a happy one, so all was good. With my nose mere inches from the mirror, I checked myself out, grateful for a smattering of gray hair I wore as a badge of honor, not a burden, because I really didn't look forward to the idea of hair dye.

I brushed my teeth again and, this time, cracked up at my reflection. As usual, I had gone overboard with the toothpaste, so it looked like I was foaming at the mouth. Very attractive. This made me giggle. Giggling was good to relieve some stress. Laughter was even better, but I was way too nervous for that.

The morning commute was a breeze, while my mind played every planned detail from proposition to celebration. It was a rare event, but I lucked out and found a parking spot not far from the station. With time to spare, I grabbed a Dunkin' Donuts dark roast with skimmed milk, settled in without too much bother, and even read a *Newsday* lying around to keep me grounded.

I got stuff done, amazingly, and Debs kept me right on track the whole time, bless her heart.

"Janalyn, you're daydreaming. Heads up."

A flying rubber band landed on my keyboard. I picked it up, completely baffled.

"Put that around your head and snap out of it," she said. "By this time tomorrow, you'll be engaged."

Her encouraging smile soothed me. Having Debs in my court significantly helped, but I couldn't allow her to get away with that crack on general principle.

I used my fingers as a slingshot, and my return volley hit her square in the middle of her forehead. I gasped at how close the rubber band made it to her eyes, but then we laughed so hard, I nearly peed myself.

"It's five," Debs said. "Now, skedaddle."

I jumped up. Debs did the honors of logging me out as I rushed to the ladies' room to change out of my business suit and into something alluring, more befitting the special occasion. It was a no-brainer that I chose the plum dress with the butterflies I had worn for our anniversary dinner, only this time with the appropriate undergarments. My mind raced with fond memories of Faith squealing with delight as she ripped off my dress, only to discover I had nothing whatsoever on underneath. I had more than surprised her and she me. We were a match made in heaven.

On my way out, I waved goodbye to Debs, but she shot up and gave me a hug. "You look great, but don't forget to ditch the sneakers for heels as soon as you get there. Keep me posted. Don't stress. Be happy, and, you know, enjoy yourself. Good luck."

I kissed her cheek, thankful she was almost as excited about this as I was. I didn't have the words to thank her. She ushered me toward the elevator and even pressed the buttons going down. I'd have done the exact same for her. As my mind was a whirlwind of anticipation, excitement and fear, I missed getting off at the lobby and had to go back up from the basement. It was a comedy of errors when the elevator then missed the lobby and landed two floors up. I finally did manage to get off on the right floor and make it outside the building.

In my exuberant state of mind, New York City sparkled before my eyes. Was I close to passing out? Why was I this nervous? As soon as I stepped onto the pavement, I thought I could feel the earth's rotation, but more likely, nervous system overload had me dizzy. Still, I envisioned the earth revolving around the sun the way I did Faith. Too corny for words, I had to admit I was beaming like a laser light. It had to be stopped, but I was too caught up to care.

Compared to the recycled air inside the office, the air outdoors was refreshing and comfortable for June. The birds sang sweeter. And where grass grew, it was greener. It was almost like I had met Faith all over again, when love was new and infatuation magnified the senses.

I nixed the smelly subway and skipped like a Looney Tune on the pavement instead, dodging crowds of clueless tourists holding long conversations in the middle of the sidewalk. The things that usually annoyed me to no end about city life somehow didn't today. It's a wonder I didn't whistle while I skipped. I received more than a few stares, but they were lucky I didn't burst into song. I enjoyed the sights and sounds of Manhattan that day in a whole new light.

Midtown flew by in my haste, and going into lower Manhattan, I sailed through Washington Square Park, greeting people of all ages, giving away free smiles to strangers as I went. As an old woman sat on a park bench feeding the pigeons at her feet, I paused to appreciate the highly underrated iridescent green and purple plumage that shimmered as the birds moved along the pavement. Pigeons mate for life, I noted, as I planned to do with Faith.

The summer heat gradually subsided as I headed toward city hall and thought how it was such a shame the state of New York still hadn't legalized same-sex marriage. How could we be still so backward in the year 2008? Never mind. I hadn't planned where we would go to be married, but Provincetown, Massachusetts held an overwhelming appeal if Faith liked the idea too.

There wasn't a cloud in the sky and zero humidity. It was the perfect day, with the promise of being the best night of my life. Anxious to be with Faith, I picked up the pace and approached the front steps of city hall in record time. After a quick glance toward City Hall Park, I checked my watch. I was prompt, as usual, but Faith hadn't arrived yet. I dabbed at my forehead with a tissue before checking my makeup in a pocket mirror. At least my mascara and eyeliner hadn't run and my lipstick was still intact, despite a wet brow that had to be the result of racing from Fifth Avenue to Chambers Street in record time.

I smoothed my dress with damp palms, smiling at the memories of Faith helping me out of the sheer plum dress and the resultant purr when she'd discovered I had nothing on underneath. The stares I received for standing alone on a crowded sidewalk in New York City sporting a salacious grin didn't bother me in the least.

But I did start pacing, and I must have checked my watch a dozen times already, for I could not wait to see the surprise on her face when I knelt down on one knee, ring in hand, and asked her to be my wife. I was so psyched about this plan, I had no idea how I had avoided ruining the secret over so many weeks of planning. But if I had bitten my tongue or cheek one more time, I would have surely needed stitches.

At first, the minutes ticked by slowly. But then, worry set in. Twenty minutes had passed, and still there was no sign of Faith. Unfortunately, phone service underground, especially in the subways, didn't work, so there was no point in calling her. I knew this, yet was about to key in her number anyway when my phone bleeped. I wasn't one of those crazy people who had chosen different ring tones for different callers so I never knew who it would be until I glanced at the number. I flipped open the phone expecting a message from Faith, but it was Debs, checking in.

> On bridge yet? Making everyone watching blush? <wink, wink> ;-)
>
> She's not here yet.
>
> No shit :-(
>
> Not helping.

I dialed Faith's number. No answer. I was about to call 911 when the scent of a familiar perfume made me want to weep: Faith had finally arrived. Nobody in the history of anybody had ever let out a bigger sigh of relief. Although she looked tired, she still was an amazing vision. If I could paint, her portrait would line famous art galleries.

I was getting giddily stupid. I went to kiss her hello, but my lips ended up brushing her hair instead. She must have showered, because she didn't smell like she'd spent the day in a busy kitchen.

"Hey, babe." I tried my best to sound casual. "You okay? I was getting so worried."

"Yes, I'm fine. I'm sorry I'm late. I left plenty of time to change, but then the subways were all screwed up."

"It doesn't matter, the main thing is that you're here now. I hope you have comfortable shoes."

"They're in the bag."

"Why not put them on?"

I waited while she kicked off her heels in favor of loafers.

"So, what's with all the secrecy?" she asked.

"No secrets. We're having dinner at Francesco's."

"It's my favorite." She smiled. "And?"

I was feeling better by the second. "And I thought we'd take a lovely stroll across the Brooklyn Bridge to watch the sunset."

"I gathered that. And?"

"And let's go, and you'll see," I said. I was ready to kneel down right there, but knew it would be so much more romantic on the bridge. "It's gorgeous out."

"That it is, and I'm with the most beautiful woman on Manhattan Island."

"Nuh-uh," I bumped her hip with mine. "I am."

"Let's not argue, but I beg to differ."

"Let's go then." I clutched at her hand. "They've reserved us a table overlooking the water. Come on. If we hurry, we can still catch the sun before it sets."

It wasn't unusual for us to walk in silence, as she was often wrapped up in thought, especially in that after-work period when she needed to switch gears, so we ventured onto the pedestrian walk and admired the view. The weather continued to be ideal for a summer evening with a delightful breeze. The sun crept toward the horizon. I snapped one photo after another until Faith threatened to throw me and my camera into the river if I didn't cut it out.

"Let's rest a minute," I suggested, while my stomach did backflips. I imagined I could feel the bridge sway, which was ridiculous, but everything made me queasy right now.

"What for? You're acting weird, more wired than after downing an entire carafe of coffee on an empty stomach."

Peering into her eyes, I ran my fingers through the soft locks on her head. "I love the way the sun brings out the highlights in your hair."

"Honestly, Janalyn, what's gotten into you?" She reached out to feel my forehead, but in one fluid moment, I snatched her hand, knelt down on one knee, and looked up at her. Her expression looked as if she would pass right out or die of embarrassment or both.

"What are you doing?" she exclaimed. "Get up, get up!"

"These past thirteen years have been the best of my life," I said. "I love you more each day. You make me the happiest woman alive. I don't ever want to live without you." I removed the ring box from my handbag and opened it. There was barely enough sun left but the street lamps made the gold and diamonds twinkle. "Faith Stacey Horowitz, will you be my wife?"

The windy day had made her long straight hair a tangled mess, and it swayed now in front of her face. But it was not enough to conceal the tightness of her lips as Faith's expression turned into one of clear horror. I had expected smiles at the very least and happy tears at most. I was not prepared for dismay.

"Janalyn…I…we. Oh, shit, what brought this on?"

Squaring her shoulders, she reached down and lifted me so that we were eye-to-eye. I couldn't speak. I couldn't cry, because the pain was so great. I couldn't even breathe. I gaped at her, waiting for her to say something as she peered into my eyes. Was that pity I saw?

"Why do we need to get married?" she finally said. "Everything is perfect as it is; a piece of paper won't change that."

"I love you, Faith. We're so good together."

"Precisely why we don't need a silly certificate that's not recognized by the majority of the country."

"I thought you'd be overjoyed. Why are you so against it?" I said simply, but dying a slow death inside. What should have been the best moment of my life was turning into a nightmare.

"Janalyn, darling, why don't we go to Francesco's and enjoy a nice romantic dinner and talk about it over an expensive bottle of wine? What do you say?"

"I can't believe you don't want to marry me." I stood there shaking but unmoving from the spot I wished would open up and let me fall through.

"It's not that. Marriage is a waste of money. It's not legal, for one, and two, what difference will a certificate make?"

"Why make excuses? If you love me as I love you, you'd marry me no matter what anyone—judge, court or country—thinks."

"Stop it, Janalyn. You're talking crazy. The main thing is that I love you and I don't need to be reminded that our love isn't recognized. Now, let me see this ring."

She examined it in the box but didn't put it on.

"Marry me anyway," I said.

She reached for my hand, but I resisted, still standing firm in my spot, as if moving meant I was living and still breathing and not in the deep recesses of a nightmare from which I could still wake up. I gave it my best shot. I don't remember why it mattered as much as it did, and I wasn't beyond pleading, but I'd never expected I'd whimper.

"Faith, I'm asking you to be my wife. Give me a better reason why not."

"I already said why: it's not legal, we're good, and there's no need to flush money down the toilet for an institution that does not include us, period."

"That's a cop-out and you know it."

"Don't push me, Janalyn."

"Marry me, then."

"No."

With my stomach twisted in knots, bile rose in my throat. This was simply not the reaction I had even contemplated, let alone one I could endure. Was this what thirteen years together had been to Faith? As good as it got?

"Tell me why, Faith; tell me the real reason. I think I have a right to know." My voice rose close to hysteria. Faith's grimace showed me she was growing weary of a conversation she clearly did not want to have, but I could not end it. I just couldn't. I pushed her and pushed her until I thought she'd blow.

"I can't marry you...because...why are you doing this, Janalyn?"

I shook her, as if trying to detach the words from her lips. Tears fell freely from my eyes, but I didn't wipe them away. "Say it, Faith. Say it, damn it!"

"I'm already married."

Her words hit me like a dump truck, and I swallowed hard to avoid losing my lunch. Married? What did that mean? For a moment, I considered turning around and leaving, running, actually; but I had to know the truth; I deserved to know. With every ounce of self-preservation and strength I had left in me after this revelation, I held her arms with an iron grip, just above her elbows. Neither she nor I would be leaving until I got answers.

"It's complicated," she said.

I waited, still too fragile to speak.

"I knew it was wrong, but when we met at Lincoln Center back then, I fell in love. I thought I could resist you—I tried and I tried, but..."

"Go on." My voice was gruff. I didn't sound anything like myself.

"I married my husband so long ago. He would contest me filing for a divorce, and honestly, I don't know if I want one. I don't know why I can't have you both."

Husband. She had a husband, whom she'd been married to before we even met.

"Stop." I covered my ears; I'd heard enough. Reality had clawed its way into my life, and the claws were tearing through my heart, ripping every part of me to teeny tiny pieces. Nothing in my entire life had ever hurt this bad. Nothing. It was like touching her burnt the flesh right off my palms.

"All I know is you lied to me," I said in an empty monotone "I can't stand the sight of you. Goodbye, Faith."

I turned to leave and didn't look back, despite the sobs I heard echoing behind me from a woman I obviously didn't know.

At one point, I stopped to stare blankly at a spectacular star-studded sky I could not in the least appreciate. Life had been so vibrant one minute, and now it was all blurred and muddled. It was as if ice ran through my veins, and I shivered from head to foot. How I didn't pass out or jump off the bridge that night was nothing short of a miracle. I walked around in a daze for hours—contemplating, unable to self-soothe. I hadn't seen this coming at all. What had happened? What had I missed? How could I have been so stupid?

When I simply could not walk one more step, I sank into an empty park bench in Washington Square Park, I think. I bawled like a baby, not far from the loitering homeless folk, who kept their distance. I cried until all my strength and will had literally run out. When a jogger stopped to ask if I was okay, I could only manage a grunting sound and a feeble nod.

With a couple of bars left on my cell phone, I finally called Debs. She got me to her apartment, held me while I cried, and medicated us both with shots and shots of whiskey.

Except to use the bathroom, I didn't even get out of her spare bed after that for a week. I couldn't eat or sleep. I holed up at Debs's place and called in sick most of that month, losing ten pounds and looking like death warmed over.

Once I emerged from my helpless state, I found that Faith had already put the house on the market. I couldn't afford to buy her out without taking a major home equity loan on the existing mortgage, nor could I bear to stay there, surrounded by memories and her scent. She removed all her stuff right away, sold, or donated our shared items. I had two weeks to figure out what I would do or where I would go. She didn't elaborate in our communications, because I would not give her the time of day anyway.

I thought I had known everything there was to know about her. I had thought I understood her. I had thought we would be together forever. But instead, the sun was gone and with it my heart. We were through; that was the easy part.

The hard part was figuring out how to get over her.

Chapter 5

Fall 2013

GODDAMN IT! NOT ANOTHER ONE of these annoying messages—the latest *happy hump day* greeting, from someone within the company who had nothing better to do than send out mass e-mails to coworkers. What was the world coming to? Correspondence these days was already a garbage heap overflowing with useless information in epic proportions! It was overwhelming just keeping up with urgent matters without having to filter through all the junk, especially junk with eye appeal. It's not like I was averse to viewing sugary sentiments depicting scantily clad voluptuous women in my inbox—quite the contrary; I enjoyed it, more than I cared to admit. But after Faith's bomb, everything had changed. I still couldn't believe it was over. A revelation that sickened me to the core and back.

The effects of the breakup were long-lasting: One stray thought about Faith in the morning could still ruin an entire day. I became annoyed by things I hadn't given a second thought to when I was settled in my personal life; a harmless random e-mail like this could set me off. But displacing my anger from Faith's betrayal into griping at the flaws of the modern-day world only made it worse, so I hit *delete* and watched the distraction disappear from the screen.

It was no use pretending to concentrate, so I propelled my chair around to pester Debs during her bouts of peak production, hoping her work ethic was contagious. It was amazing that she never missed a beat, even with my interruptions. I poked my head around the partition between us. She smacked the keyboard, at times with one hand, turning pages with the other. Other papers went flying as she entered information.

"Sheesh, Debs! You type like a speed demon. I can't delete spam as fast as that. Speaking of…I'm drowning in hump day greetings gone viral, not to mention tons of ads, dating sites I didn't sign up for…need I go on? How do you keep up?"

"You're either Miss Popularity, or your e-mail address has been hacked. Time for a new identity. Let me finish up here, and I'll re-assign you a new e-mail—something easy to remember but impossible to abuse."

With the prospect of this problem going away forever, I had to admit that a part of me liked some of these junk mails. But I had to stop ogling women who didn't exist, I told myself. I rolled my chair back behind my desk. As if my computer had heard me, a glittery photo of a voluptuous bare-breasted fairy with wings large enough for two showed up on my screen, luring me in. Her come-hither smile and enormous eyes inviting me to fly away with her made a certain part of my anatomy clench, reminding me that its neglect was bordering on detrimental to my health. One look at this imaginary woman had me hot to pack it all in and head directly to fairyland.

Damn Faith for leaving me so desperate. These photos were constant reminders of what I was missing. It had me interminably depressed, cynical and with a low tolerance for minor inconveniences.

I didn't have long to obsess before Patrick, who appeared to have aged significantly and was back to work not long after bypass surgery, headed my way. He'd enrolled in a medically supervised fitness regime, but in my humble opinion, he still had a ways to go before he was out of the woods, where his health was concerned. When he arrived at my desk, I practically knocked the escape key right off my keyboard in my rush to close the naughty picture, fearing any sudden rise in his blood pressure might land him back in the hospital.

"Hey, Patrick. What's up?"

"Janalyn, do you mind figuring a way to use these handouts when you get a chance? Spruce 'em up a bit. Syd, the autocratic administrative pain in the rectum, is on my back."

It was hysterical to hear Patrick speak this way, but I didn't want to offend him by laughing. And rectum summed him up nicely.

I shifted a stack of papers to one side of my desk to make room for more, glancing briefly at the cover of the brochures. The outfits the models wore showed how outdated they were. I'd have to start from scratch, which I figured was what Patrick had in mind all along, the sly devil.

"Sure thing," I said, since I didn't really mind, "drop them here."

"Thanks, kiddo, if anyone can do it justice, you're the one."

"No prob." I smiled at him, wondering if he was getting laid regularly, possibly even against medical advice. The very idea that everyone was having sex but me, whether or not it was true, turned my smile to an instant frown. Since when had I become so pitiful?

Time to move on. I picked up where I had left off after Patrick had disrupted my fragile concentration. Too soon afterward, a random newspaper clipping with a photo of a beautiful woman landed on my keyboard from the other side of the partition, so Debs had to be the culprit; I tossed it aside, not amused. Every stinking thing these days oozed sex appeal. Even Scott Spencer Enterprises ads were guilty of exploiting the adage "sex sells." I couldn't escape it. If I didn't nurture myself soon, I feared my libido would wither and die.

But Debs was going to ask me about it soon, so I reluctantly looked at the photo. It was none other than a publicity snapshot of Victoria Beckham. *Somebody should send her food aid*, I thought. My idea of sexy had a bit more cushion on them bones. But then, my idea of sexy had also been purely theoretical, past history, five excruciating years ago, to be exact. There hadn't been anyone—ever—after Faith. Pathetic.

In spite of starving herself skinny, Victoria was attractive in that charismatic way that was impossible to deny. But clearly, Debs didn't like her, because it was obvious that she had cut the former Spice Girl out of a picture with her husband; all that was left of soccer god David Beckham was a part of his arm draped over her bare shoulder. As I examined the picture, I heard Debs's unmistakable giggle.

I glanced up to find her looking down at me from the other side of my cubicle with my clearly labeled *hands off* scissors in hand. Sporting a huge grin, she held the rest of David Beckham's photo close to her heart.

"Pretty please, Janalyn, be a pal. You take Victoria so I can have David all to myself."

"You do realize that Posh Spice and David Beckham have four children together? Better leave this one alone," I suggested. "And please put the scissors back where you found them."

In response, Debs pouted flirtatiously, crumbled the picture of Mrs. Beckham into a ball, and promptly shot it into the wastebasket. "I *was* going to give you a new e-mail addy, but it can wait."

She then made a major production of putting my scissors in my personal stash canister and sauntered back to her cubicle, grumbling. "All I asked was for help distracting Victoria so I can have a night with my heartthrob."

I yawned and stretched, as much as my office chair allowed, when I caught a part of the *Daily News* Debs hadn't butchered. *What a bummer*, I smirked: Faith's favorite Latin group was disbanding after the lead singer allegedly ran off with their manager and all the profits.

Pain still pierced my heart at the tiniest reminder of Faith; this huge knot in my stomach made me nauseous. When would I ever get over the fact that our relationship had been a farce? I should be glad, right? Better we were done, kaput, so I didn't waste another minute of my life on something that never was real. Thirteen wasted years had been enough.

Get over it, Janalyn. As if I hadn't punished myself plenty with repetitive recriminations, I pinched my thigh through durable dress slacks of heavy-gauge cotton and man-made elastane, which was not satisfying at all, but it beat the hell out of picking my skin until it bled or eating my way into a hot fudge sundae coma. No matter how many times I told myself that I was better off without the lying would-be polygamist, I couldn't get over Faith. I found it hard to forget and impossible to forgive. There were days when I resorted to mean thoughts, acting like an errant child calling her bad names. But digressions from maturity did nothing to placate my battered soul. *Melodrama* soon replaced Melody as my middle name, when I wasn't mentally shut down from maintaining my stony façade.

I was determined never again to open myself up the way I did with Faith, stubbornly refusing myself too much happiness. If I was going to bleed, it would be the result of my own hands, not someone I trusted implicitly. Yes, I'd become bitter, no fun at all, but at least I was safe. One afternoon, I had gone shopping with my mother and nearly bit her head off just because she'd dared turn on the radio in her own car. The love songs on every channel my mother flipped to made me want to bolt out of the car in the middle of the highway.

Poor Mom. Faith had hurt her little girl. It didn't matter that I was all grown up; she had never been able to stand me getting even a small "booboo," as she called every scratch and scrape I'd ever had. Emotional turmoil put her over a freaking cliff. That day in the car, she had told me, "You're only as happy as your most miserable child; remember that, Janalyn."

"Thanks, Mom. I needed a hefty portion of guilt with my sorrow today." I immediately regretted my words.

"That's not what I meant. I just want you to be happy."

I patted her right hand that had drifted off the wheel and onto the car seat. "It's okay, Mom, I know." But by the time we had parked the car as far away from the nearest entrance as possible, I had forgotten why we had ventured to the mall in the first place, and I was already stressing over the crowds. Material goods were the last things on earth that could lift my spirits. I had not owned anything like that since Faith's necklace gift to me and the ring I had bought to propose to her. When I had given Faith back the diamond necklace and took a substantial loss on selling the engagement ring, my only thought had been *good riddance*. I didn't want anything more from Faith, even though that had left me still without a home.

Lucky for me, Debs had a two-bedroom apartment, a throwback from her rent-sharing days, but I really couldn't impose for too long. After a couple of months, despite Debs insisting she loved my company, I went back to my childhood home, but quickly found my old bedroom, not to mention trying to appear upbeat so as not to upset my parents, stifling beyond belief. Mom meant well, but she was overbearing, and her incessant worrying and fussing over me drove me crazy. I soon needed my own space.

The last time I had set eyes on Faith was at the closing of our house. I can't remember much from that day, except how hard it was not to cry in an airless boardroom surrounded by strangers—all of them—including Faith. I didn't even reach out to her when she wiped away a tear. If her heart was broken nearly half as badly as mine, then good—she deserved it. I used my half of the money, not much, since we had had a huge mortgage, to finally rent my own place in the city. Aside from personal effects, my computer, and Grandma's silver, I took very little with me, avoiding reminders, and bought brand-new furnishings for my new life.

I continued to beat myself up for being blind, but I still was desperately in love with Faith. I hated like hell to think that I was. Only a complete moron would have any warm feelings after all that.

Even five years later, I simply could not stop the endless loop, the broken record, call it what you will, of self-destructive thoughts and behaviors once they'd started. My thoughts were like a chronic illness without hope of a cure.

At least the behaviors lessened as the years wore on. There was a time, closer to the beginning, when I had burned the candle at both ends, working like a lunatic in order to forget. Back then, I had cried as many gallons as the New York waterworks. Such a blubbering mess was not a pretty sight.

Debs never gave up on trying to snap me back to life; she was my saving grace. As an incentive to stay engaged with the world, she found a special two-for-one deal, the first month free, on an exclusive gym with membership by invitation only. We split the savings and upgraded from the YMCA to the Buttkiss Sport Spa, Midtown Manhattan's best-kept secret and with the silliest name too. Each night, we exercised long and hard, which Debs claimed was to get our money's worth, but I knew she was working hard to keep me too busy for the luxury of a good cry. She'd been right to push: hard physical and mental workouts helped pulverize the pain. I was only okay as long as I didn't stop, because the moment I took a breather, I was overwhelmed with sadness. And despite her efforts, I didn't sleep well and often woke up troubled, disoriented from vivid images; it was impossible at first to decipher whether or not they were real. Debs and I grew closer still. We'd both seen each other through horrible breakups now, and we knew how to get each other through. It baffled me to no end that Debs was still single, frankly. In my mind she was the perfect mate, and not just for her beauty alone. Sure, she was gorgeous, but she was also smart, funny and faithful to a fault. A winning combination.

Our anniversary of joining Buttkiss fell on a Friday. We planned to mark the anniversary of our joining the club with a marathon workout, followed by splurging on whatever treats we desired afterwards. Debs and I were all set to leave work on time and start our weekend off with endurance exercises, followed by a swim, if we had spare energy. I emptied out my briefcase, except for a bottle of water and bran bar, when Debs peered over the partition separating our desks.

"Are you ready for the workout of your life?" Debs's eagerness was contagious. Better to steer clear if you didn't want to get carried away. She could turn the dullest day into a party, while still managing to complete what needed to get done.

"You bet. You?"

"Absolutely. Just hitting the little girl's room, and we're off."

I bid farewell to co-workers on the way to meet Debs by the elevator. It was easy to leave, given who we worked for and what the company's principles were. Scott Spencer would have to do without their most dedicated employees for one weekend.

"My bag feels awfully light without the contents of a file cabinet in it. Why, then, am I not plagued with guilt?" I asked.

"Stop it. Let's do this without another thought."

We linked arms and headed out of the skyscraper, onto the busy streets of Manhattan, chatting the whole way.

"You really should stop printing and schlepping every piece of paper. It's why we have computers with tons of storage, you know," Debs said.

"Old habits."

The way into Buttkiss was on the side of a building that had a row of storefronts—it could easily be a service entrance, as it was unmarked and not very well lit. We had to walk down steep steps and, once inside, back up more stairs to the reception desk. It looked like a real dive from the outside.

The reception desk was manned, but we still had to swipe our photo-ID cards. The receptionist, Mandy, was busy texting, tweeting, or whatever she did at check-in and barely glanced at the screen when we swiped our cards. We walked into the locker room to the familiar scent of white linen from the room deodorizers that regularly sprayed chemicals into the air. Quickly, we changed into workout gear.

Debs was the hottest member at Buttkiss, in her black Spandex pants and her matching top, anklets and trainers, and received the most looks. I was glad to let her take the spotlight. I was there to pump iron and do some cardio, not make a fashion statement.

"Where do you want to start the warm-up?" she asked.

"Bikes. We started on treadmills last time and really should mix it up."

"You're the boss."

"Right this way," I said. "We could take a spinning class."

"Nah, not tonight. Let's go it on our own, and the first one to poop out buys the hot fudge sundaes."

"Those are mighty high stakes." I grinned. "You're on."

"What is this I hear about hot fudge?" A smooth deep baritone that reminded me of a young James Earl Jones caught our attention.

"Hey Jase." I bumped knuckles with Jason Mann. He practically owned the place. I wouldn't hesitate to bet that he was a silent partner. Jase's toned bulk spoke volumes about how many hours he invested weekly to achieve his "muscle man of the year award" look. Most folks wouldn't want to meet him in a dark alley, but I knew him as this gentle giant with a huge smile and a heart to match. I often found Debs's gaze glued to his gluteus maximus.

"Sup?" he said.

"It's our anniversary of becoming members of this joint," I said.

"Cool. You get to work out extra hard then."

"Hey, Jase, looking good," Debs said, her expression all dreamy and looking very focused on the object of her desire.

"Not as good as you," he replied. I literally had to pull Debs away, or we'd never get past check-in. Good thing she regrouped effortlessly.

"We'll do ten minutes on the bike for legs and head to rowing for upper body. Let's circuit," she said, her head back in the game.

"Sure thing."

The workout was grueling. Debs went off to take a quick break while I carried on. Jason joined me for some squats with free weights—they didn't really make dumbbells heavy enough for him, but he humored me by grunting. His wide grin gave him away. I punched his arm and nearly broke my knuckles.

"I think my friend has her eye on you," I said between lunges.

"Debs is hot, no doubt about that, but she's not my type."

I raised an eyebrow. "Debs is everyone's type."

Jason cocked his head toward the bench press to look at a white guy I had seen around a lot lately. The pale Adonis had streaked blond hair, blue eyes and a baby face that must have inspired utter devotion from the women in his family. With a photogenic physique not in need of fancy touch-up programs, he was a fine specimen of the human male. I may be a true lesbian, but I could still appreciate prime humans at their peak, and gender didn't enter into the equation. This guy was super-duper fit but not bulky like my friend Jason.

The light bulb went off in my head. How could I have been so blind? I looked up into Jason Mann's beautiful dark-skinned face and stood there mute before I could speak.

"*He's* your type? You shitting me?"

"No shit."

"He's cute, I'll give him that. Is he gay?"

"I hope so. Yeah, he's into me, I got vibes."

How the hell hadn't I known Jase was gay? I made a mental note to have my gaydar checked at the next inspection. Maybe I had a wire loose or something.

When Debs came back, she turned a bright shade of pink the closer she got to me and Jason. I thought she'd swoon from the effects of his smile. Lucky for them both, Jason was summoned to spot the blond Adonis on the weights and left, hiding his eagerness to answer the man's beck and call.

"Well, I'll be damned," I said after Jason was out of earshot.

Debs looked away the moment I peered into her eyes. "You like him," I remarked.

"I do not!"

"She who protests too much—"

"Don't be ridiculous. I think he's taken." Debs pouted; her voice even sounded deflated. "Believe me, I tried, but he, well, he wasn't interested." I wished I could whisk her hurt away. She was such a dear friend.

Actually, maybe I could help. "Do you still want to swim?"

"Nah, I think we've done more than enough, but I will if you want to."

"I agree, we're more than done here. Let's go back into the stairwell, bring a mat."

As soon as we were alone and sitting on the mats, ready for the cool down stretches, I turned to face her. "About Jase. Can I let you in on a little secret?"

"He's totally and completely in love with me too?" Debs asked, ever hopeful.

"Sorry, babe, but you are definitely not his type. He prefers pretty boys, preferably blonde and buff."

Debs looked as if every sweet dream she'd ever had turned sour. "Sorry," I said.

"Not your fault. I just can't believe it. Why are the good ones always taken or gay?"

"I don't have a clue."

"It's so sad that he feels he has to keep his sexual orientation so well hidden. How did you find out?" she asked. She was already onto curious questions, moving on past her heartbreak. I had to applaud her resilience.

"He told me."

"Why would he do that?"

"I may not flaunt it, but I sure as hell don't keep my preferences a secret. Jase never uttered a disparaging word or went all quiet like some people do whenever the topic of homosexuality arises. When you're part of a minority, Debs, you remember this sort of thing and you file it away in your head for later. While things have improved in general, some folks still act as if it rips their comfort zone to shreds."

"It's a shame. I don't think anyone should have to hide. I'm proud of you that you don't."

"I know."

"You're my favorite lesbian."

"Oh, so now you're collecting us?"

"No, silly. I still love Ellen and Melissa, but I love you most of all."

"Thanks."

We did our cool down reps effortlessly. I felt invigorated, like I could conquer the world.

"Neither of us pooped out first, so who buys the decadent dessert?" she asked.

"I say we skip it. I feel too good to ruin it with a sugar hangover tomorrow."

"Me too. Let's share a smoothie at the juice bar after showers instead."

"Deal."

We rarely missed a workout.

While it took a long time to function again normally, I had eventually become the model employee. I arrived early, worked late, hardly ate, skipped breaks, and threw myself into more projects than a sane person could handle on her best day. In other words, I was all work and no play. The extra cash from a hefty bonus was the result. Money doesn't guarantee happiness, it doesn't erase painful experiences, and it doesn't keep you company at night, but it helps with the bills. I was able to afford a slightly larger apartment in a better part of the city.

Patrick came by again. "Do you by any chance have the monthly report yet?"

"Yes, it's right here. I just need to look it over once more, and it's yours."

"No e-mail, please. I prefer the printed form."

"You got it." Patrick didn't trust computers, not having grown up with them. Once on paper, as opposed to reading on-screen, I viewed my latest report with fresh eyes.

The most surprising result of my research was the finding that employees who perceived that their company, and in particular their immediate supervisors, actually cared about their health took far less sick days, regardless of whether or not they participated in the "Go Health, Reap the Wealth" program. Most people didn't want or need to be told to go on a diet, to exercise, and to give up smoking. I was like most people. Tell me what to do, and I was more likely to do the opposite; I was affected more by personal motivation than outside influence. At least we instructed CEOs to allow for extra time, supplies, information, and incentives to entice employees to adopt better habits.

Good thing I hadn't handed my report to Patrick earlier. After a morning spent in personal musings of the negative kind, some of the wording in my discussions and conclusions looked like they were written by a bitter woman. I toned it down considerably, vying for more upbeat descriptions where improvements were warranted, and then printed out the final version. Quite pleased with my revision, I dropped a copy on Patrick's desk. Then I scribbled a note to Debs on a paper airplane and watched while it flew over the center divider. I heard her chuckle and smiled, despite myself.

Debs wheeled her ergonomic chair backward to peek into my cubicle while aiming my paper airplane at the center of my forehead.

I held my hands up in surrender. "Hold on there. Just wondering if you're gymming tonight."

"Of course, you?"

"Count me in."

Debs turned swiftly to look into the distance behind her. "Psssssssst, Jana! Don't look now, but here comes double trouble."

I closed Wikipedia faster than a blink of an eye, but opening a Word document was a different story. I tapped on the table next to my mouse in a restless, rhythmic motion, but then had to stretch up to peer over the partition and across the office, unable not to look. Debs waved me back down.

"There's some talk about restructuring. I have no idea what that's about. Heads down, maybe they'll torment someone else," she hissed.

I plunked down into my chair with more of a thump than intended. At least Scott Spencer, our fine founder, was a total mensch in every sense of the word. He possessed integrity and honor, measuring well above mere mortals, and was part of the reason Debs and I lasted as his employees twenty-three years and counting. But the sound of Marcus, our relentless acting chief, coming straight for my head with his snooty assistant, Cynthia, made my heart speed up with stress. After a whole song and dance, my computer did me the honors and finally reopened my latest file. It was pristine, but I could always find something to tweak.

"Janalyn, upstairs, now," Marcus said, his tone, as ever, clipped, condescending, and just plain rude. I was old enough to be his mother and would have loved reminding him to wipe his nose and watch his tone or there'd be consequences, but knew better than to piss him off. Never an explanation, permission, or pleasantry was uttered from his lips. I'd put up with him since he'd finished his MBA—most probably in Dictatorship—for over two years now.

"Janalyn!"

"Excuse me, sir? Where?" To his face, I called him "sir". On bad days, Debs and I called him Mucous behind his back.

"Follow me."

I wiped my damp palms on my trousers and steadied my knees as I stood. Upstairs was where senior employees had their appraisals, were written up, or were fired. *Oh shit, now what?*

"You too, Deborah. Both of you bring your things. You won't be coming back to your desks after the meeting."

Debs and I exchanged puzzled, bordering on worried, glances before grabbing our bags and suit jackets. I was sure we were going to face the firing squad and wondered if we'd at least be offered a last meal or statement. We signed off our computers, locked our desks, all as usual, but in complete, foreboding silence.

Marcus uncharacteristically opened the heavy door to a conference room, and shockeroo, he held it, allowing Debs and I to enter first. His crooked smile was as close to pleased as I think it ever got. There were three remaining seats at a huge mahogany table, where the man himself, Scott Spencer, sat discussing something with another executive.

Debs and I looked at each other. Senior Spencer rarely came into work unless something important was happening. What did this mean? We then returned our attention to the entire executive board. This did not look like a disciplinary hearing but rather a department head convergence. What was going on? Not letting them see me sweat, I kept my jacket on.

Despite over two decades at the same company, including more than a few promotions, I had never been in the main boardroom throughout my total employ. I sat in the firm but comfy chair and glanced down at my suit, thankful for having worn the tweed jacket and dress slacks. I looked sharp, if I did say so myself. Debs had on a dark jacket and matching skirt that hugged her figure in all the right places, but then, she was the kind of woman who would look great in a shopping bag. She was truly a stunning woman, but thankfully, without airs. An amazing combination in my humble opinion. But none of this would help us if we were about to be fired.

It was still too soon to relax and enjoy the invite. Deep in prayer for something good on the horizon, I had to remember to breathe. The buzz in the boardroom thrummed through my veins. Excited murmurs from the people in the room ricocheted off thick paneled walls and onto the floor-to-ceiling windows, only to be absorbed in the plush carpeting. I couldn't make out what anyone was saying, and I didn't have much time to appreciate views of Manhattan rivaling the Empire State Building observatory before all noise instantly ceased, as the senior Mr. Spencer signaled Junior Spencer to begin.

"We're assembling a team for our first world health initiative," Marcus said in a measured style, as if weighing each word and paying per syllable. "As some of you may know, the healthcare crisis is clearly out of hand, costing billions, where demand has far exceeded supply of practitioners, hospitals, nursing care facilities, and home healthcare agencies, and has left too many without medical care at all." He rattled off figures I knew by heart, since I was the one who provided them.

"Here at Scott Spencer Enterprises, our aim has always been to work within a specific target population—the needs of employed adults and their employers. Our new vision is to expand to a larger demographic. There's a healthcare crisis, people. I won't belabor a point of which we are all too well aware, but poor lifestyle choices have greatly increased the incidence of morbity and premature mortality, which has burdened an already overwhelmed industry. Private and public healthcare systems simply cannot cope with the glut. Let's take obesity, for example: the incidence is at epidemic proportions—and in areas of the world where it was hardly a concern before.

"Our figures show we have the expertise to set up programs that attack the problem at the ground level, and that there's much to be gained by joining forces with European firms. We've been reorganizing our workforce to accommodate a shift in responsibilities. Six of you have been invited here to work together on the project, but only two candidates have been selected to travel to a pilot conference we're arranging in the United Kingdom this summer. In front of you, you'll find packets with all the information you'll need to get started."

I fingered the thick, sealed manila envelope, itching to rip it open.

"You'll all be expected to network with our new international colleagues via e-mails, but the two attendees will speak and chair at least one panel discussion in your area of expertise. If the project meets with success as projected, more man-hours will be allocated abroad. Dim the lights, please, Cynthia. Now, I ask you all to give your undivided attention to the short slide presentation on what we hope to accomplish in the coming years."

As the lights dimmed, Marcus was downright chatty for once. "As I've already mentioned, the board has already selected two out of the six people I've invited here today and pending the agreement of those candidates, we'll move forward," he said.

My mind wandered, despite efforts to stay focused. It was so good to thrum for a good reason for a change. A two-out-of-six chance that either Debs or I would get a trip to the UK—those odds weren't dreadful. And even the one-in-fifteen odds that both of us would get to go together were pretty decent.

I glanced around the room to size up the competition, half men and half women. Debs and I stole excited glances and mouthed, "Cool!" before returning our attention to the screen.

A question-and-answer session followed the presentation. At five o'clock sharp, we were dismissed with a huge information packet to commit to memory. Marcus looked directly at me. It was odd, but rather than shrink, I lengthened my spine, gave him my commanding pose, and thought I detected a spark of interest in his eyes.

"Go home, think about it and I'd like your decisions regarding participation. The deadline is Friday, I'm afraid, as we would like to get started as early as the following Monday. Goodnight ladies and gentlemen. You have a lot to mull over. We've chosen you for a reason. You won't let us down. Thank you. Dismissed."

I was still in shock about being invited, but who had been selected to travel remained a mystery.

"I don't want to open it here, do you?" Debs put an arm around mine for moral support.

I had a hysterical giggle in my throat ready to erupt with embarrassing consequences, so I held onto Debs for dear life and she to me as we headed out of the building arm-in-arm. First, the relief of not being fired, then the possibility of representing our company across the pond was almost more than my nervous system could bear. I was too scared to find out which two lucky souls should pack their bags.

At one point, during the supersonic elevator trip down to the lobby, Debs laced her fingers through mine and tightly squeezed them until I smiled at her. I weighed the possibilities in my mind: The Spencers had to pick us to fly to the UK. Debs and I would be their very best bet; I had no doubt about that! Two unattached career-minded women who knew how to get the job done was just what they needed at this convention.

Once we hit the crowded, and I mean jam-packed streets of Midtown, Debs's bubble of excitement exploded: "O-M-F-G, England!"

"I am so on the same page, Debs!"

"Unbelievable." She squeezed the envelope until her fingers visibly blanched. "We have to open it, but I'm too scared."

"Let's get somewhere private first, just in case." I looked around. Manhattan was teeming with commuters in the midst of Midtown rush hour. "Not here, but where?"

"I have no idea but we'll figure it out," she said. "We are so going to England, right?"

"Damn right."

"You know, Debs," I said, dodging speed-walkers like a steel ball in a pinball machine, "I just realized I haven't left the office during rush hour in five years. I can't get over the number of people per square mile."

"You mean per square inch! It's worse now than during lunchtime." Debs zigzagged as she walked.

"Speaking of...Get a load of the aroma of Manhattan's finest cuisine: hot dogs, fried onions and sauerkraut, giant pretzels, and, oh God, I've got to resist those candied nuts that's making my mouth water."

"You know what I'm realizing?" Debs said. "I can't remember you this elated in a long time, nor this ravenous that you'd care for food from a street van. It's such a relief."

We were soon lost in our own thoughts. In general, New Yorkers spent a lot of time trying to steer clear of the irate speed-walker to avoid being knocked down. Ignoring the incessant beggar was another art. The same with not falling prey to the street seller, or refusing to gather up umpteen useless leaflets being shoved in faces.

"There's a lot to be said for working late," Debs said, stepping over the paw of a guide dog while his owner was fingering a bunch of loose change in his hat.

"True," I said. "Less congestion, anyway, but you know, Debs? Something has just occurred to me."

"Yeah, what's that?"

"I never minded working late, and I have never been a fan of jostling crowds. But I actually love the sights, smells, sounds, and the hustle and bustle of New York City, I really do."

It was an epiphany of sorts. I hadn't known until that moment how much I took living in Manhattan for granted. I liked my apartment. It was in walking distance to Midtown, but not in the thick of it. While I enjoyed living on Long Island, New York City felt closer to home than I'd come in a long time. I had to get out and enjoy the city more often, take in more shows, picnic in the park, visit museums all over again, shop until I dropped.

After we had sold the property and gone our separate ways, I often wondered if it was the house or Faith that I missed most. I did miss a lot of things about not living there any longer, but there were many advantages to living in the city: There were more interesting restaurants, more cultural pursuits, more shopping, and every amenity one could imagine, all easily accessible. And the incessant sirens outside my windows at all hours of the day and night actually helped me forget the memories that taunted me in the night. Not to mention my current address beat the commute into the city, because I was already there.

Are you listening to me at all, Janalyn?"

"Huh?"

"I'll get to see David Beckham," she said.

"David Beckham? Urm..." I stalled to catch up with her conversation. "I think he lives in LA, doesn't he?"

She shrugged. "I have no idea."

"Some fan you are." I laughed at her enthusiasm, but actually, I was a closet starstruck girl too, with an arsenal of idols—surprisingly many of them British. I wouldn't mind meeting Cate Blanchett, Emma Thompson, Helen Mirren and Kate Winslet. Heck, I'd go nuts meeting Judi Dench. I loved her in *Skyfall* and *Casino Royale*. And these were just the women, but Debs interrupted me before my brain could get to the male ones.

"Who do you think they picked?"

"Your guess is as good as mine, but I would say we're the ones that they want."

"How do you figure that?"

"We dress sharp." I held up my thumb and began ticking off our attributes. "We're smart, we're goal oriented, outspoken, and we're single. We make a solid team. Noooooooooo distractions."

"You forgot to mention super-duper at multitasking."

"Multitasking?" I asked, but already knew the answer. Debs's sly smile gave her away every time.

"Mixing business with pleasure. We get the job done and celebrate afterwards."

"You are a talented multitasker. If we're chosen, I plan to see things through. You can have your own parties."

"Don't be such a spoil sport."

"Oh God, I'm dying to know already."

"Me too." I shook the packet as if it would give us a clue to the contents, which of course it didn't. "Want to grab some dinner before we look, so we don't spoil my appetite? It's amazing to desire food for a change."

"Good idea. We eat, then we rip open the envelopes, and come what may, everything is going to be okay. I'm sure you'll miss me plenty if I go without you."

"Excuse me—who said anything about them choosing you instead of *moi*? It could be the other way around, you know."

"I know, I hope we both get it. Please let us be the chosen ones, please."

"Amen."

"Dinner first sounds like a plan. Lead on."

We picked up the pace, quickly shopping for a few groceries to cook up for supper. The second we stepped into Debs's apartment, the temptation to find out what those envelopes contained bowled us over. Unable to resist a second longer, we sat on the sofa together and ripped open the envelopes on the count of three. Debs held her eyes shut. I peered inside my packet first.

Skipping over *Dear Miss Jacobs,* I immediately zoned in on *Congratulations* before the meaning of the word registered in my brain. Was I being congratulated on being selected to just work on the project or was I going to England as well? That was the question.

"What does yours say? Give it here!" Debs took the papers right out of my hands, quickly scanned them, dropping pages as she digested them. I sat motionless. It seemed an eternity but then she dropped the whole damn packet as she grabbed me in a boa-constricting hug.

"We're both going to *bloomin'* England!" she said in an exaggerated British accent if ever I heard one.

I laughed so hard, I couldn't stop until we were jumping, hugging and crying all at once.

"We're going out to celebrate," I said.

"You've got that right." Debs raised her palm for a high five. "Let's go."

The next day at work, it was like Debs and I were walking on air. I couldn't say who was beaming brighter. Of course, the first thing we did was accept the positions as lead ambassadors of the global healthcare initiative. I loved the sound of our new titles and found Marcus as pleased for us as we were for ourselves. We both left his office that day with a spring in our step. We skipped lunch, too excited to eat, and delved into calling a team meeting for that afternoon.

There was so much to do, excitement was all the fuel we needed. I swiftly placed a fresh cup of coffee on Debs's desk fifteen minutes before our meeting. She mumbled thanks, but didn't look up.

The plans I mapped out that morning were shaping up nicely. "How's it going on your end?" I asked Debs. "Have you typed up the tentative schedule and assignments we talked about last night?"

"Sure did. Let's get everyone together." She gathered up the loose papers that were littering her desk, tapped them twice to straighten the pages, and was ready to go.

As we walked down the hall to find an empty meeting room, Debs and I chatted. "I've never been off the continental United States, except for Hawaii, which doesn't count," I said, as my brainwaves fired every which way.

"Canada doesn't count as going abroad and I've been there lots of times. So me neither," she said.

"Any clue why they chose to hold the pilot conference in, of all places, Southwest Devon rather than London?"

"My guess, cost. They don't want to spend more in case it doesn't pan out. Venues in major cities charge a fortune to hold conferences."

"That's what I thought. After I got home last night, I was too excited to sleep, so I did an intensive Devon search. I've already decided we're going to delve right in and see as many sights as possible."

"Funnily enough, I too looked it up. I wouldn't mind hitting a few National Trust or English Heritage properties. Besides all that, the history alone could keep me endlessly amused."

"I'm most definitely hiking the moors. I might go bird watching if I have time. Whoever chose Devon gets high praise from me." I opened and held the door for Debs.

We entered the room to find the whole gang already there, including Patrick, who I could tell was gearing up to give a formal and highly unnecessary opening speech to our meeting.

"I'd like to extend heartfelt congratulations on behalf of all gathered here today to Janalyn and Debs for being selected to represent the firm," said Patrick. "I have no doubt they are very well suited for the job—"

"Congratulations to us all," I interjected, before Patrick got too carried away. The man loved the sound of his own voice. I hadn't overlooked the fact that Debs and I were chosen instead of him, seeing how he was the employee with the longest work record, but there was no time to belabor the thought. I had a lot of points to cover.

"We have six months to prepare, which sounds like enough time, but in fact, with all our other duties, fitting in extra responsibilities will take finagling." I glanced around the room, suddenly aware that I was standing, and promptly sat down, preferring to maintain level eye contact.

"As your leader, I want to stress that this is a team effort, and we are all on equal footing. If anything needs addressing, it's up to all of us to bring it up. I've put together a tentative list I know you'll all want to fine-tune. On a personal note, Debs and I wish you were all invited to the convention, but know that your presence will be with us every step of the way."

In less than two hours, we had drawn a viable working schematic, agreeable to all, that detailed designated responsibilities.

"I vote Patrick in charge of overall organization," I said. "Who seconds the motion?"

All hands shot up, unanimously everyone agreed. Patrick beamed at the vote. I could tell he was delighted to be named chief-in-charge, a position I knew he'd claim no matter what, so I had figured why not make it official? We then decided to make Debs in charge of all correspondence between us and the delegates all over the world.

So far, so good. Nobody said 'boo,' so I continued, turning my attention to Neil, a wiry man in his late twenties with shoulder-length golden brown hair. "As Neil is our computer whiz and amazing at graphics, it's a no-brainer that he should head all the artwork and technical stuff to make us look sharp during our presentations." His tentative smile and nod was adorable. Debs was protective of him because he reminded her of Dr. Spencer Reed on *Criminal Minds*, and he *was* adorable when he smiled. But I could see why he wasn't going to the United Kingdom.

"Fern should be in charge of research, editing and the final proofreading of anything before it goes to print,"

Patrick said. I was genuinely surprised that he had managed to stay silent this long.

I knew Fern quite well. She liked to talk about herself and did just that at every opportunity. There wasn't a soul who didn't know that she had a graduate degree in English Literature with a minor in Dramatic Arts, and that she had aced both, naturally. We had all been invited to attend the comedy club where she did stand-up too. As my editor, she was able to tweak my composition in such a way that even I was amazed at how smart and witty I sounded after all was said and done, and she had a wicked sense of humor. But her most valuable skill on this project was that she was a pro at training staff in public speaking. One session with Fern and you'd be cured of saying, "Um, er, or ah," or else.

"I'll be around for the dress rehearsals if you need," Fern said.

Debs smirked. "We need," she said. "Promise you'll get Janalyn to slow down, enunciate and not go off on too many tangents and you'll get huge praise from me."

I cast a sideways glance at Debs, but didn't get into it with her.

"One last point: Debs has taken minutes today, but we need someone to do it regularly. Any takers?"

Patrick and Fern's hands shot up at the same time. "I'll leave it to you two to decide. You can take turns, whatever, as long as I have something to hand Marcus after the meeting."

We adjourned with everyone on the same page. It was helpful that there weren't any hard feelings where Debs and I were concerned. Having Patrick in our court had set the tone. The other three members did not gripe about being passed over for the travel, at least not in our presence.

Debs and I were the last to leave the room. I turned off the lights, feeling brighter than I had in years. This new challenge took my mind off introspection. It was already proving to be rewarding, and we were only getting started. Just wait until Debs and I landed on British soil.

"Look out dear sweet United Kingdom of Great Britain and Northern Ireland," I said to Debs. "Janalyn Melody Jacobs and Deborah Foster-Baker are headed your way." If my grin was any wider, the corners of my mouth would reach my ears.

Debs grinned back. "Heaven help the Brits then."

Day One had flown by at top speed. Only one hundred sixty one days left to go.

Our lives had become filled with routine: Marcus left us memo after memo, but with our exuberance, even he couldn't succeed in pissing us off. We were nearly there. I wrote a report detailing the harsh statistics, interventions, outcomes, and what we were doing in America to address the obesity crisis within major corporations. I explained how our strategies might be applied to the entire population with the long-term goal being cutting healthcare costs. Debs concentrated on what we could bring to Europe, how business leaders in both the U.S. and Europe could work together and find ways to improve the lifestyle choices of the general public.

Fern had me recite my presentation until my throat was sore, but to her credit, I had memorized my spiels and delivered my lines with better diction than I had ever thought possible. She was a miracle worker. When she was certain Debs and I were ready, she let Patrick and Neil have their final say before announcing to us all that the full dress rehearsal was scheduled.

"We can have access to an empty conference room, fully equipped, anytime you want," Neil said.

"Good work, Neil," Patrick said. "Tomorrow at ten sharp we meet to tape the girls' presentations. Fern can fine-tune anything that doesn't work."

"Pat, that's fine, but we'll need any staff you can gather to act as our audience participation," Debs added.

"Already done," he said. "You'll have everyone on hand. I also took the liberty to plant questions, so be sure to allow ample time for Q and A."

"No problem, we're all set," I said, glancing over at Debs, who nodded. I then turned my attention back to the whole group. "Any questions?"

All the heads shook *no*. I treated them all to my most inspiring smile.

"All right, then. If there isn't anything else, let's go over it one more time," I announced. "From the top."

Chapter 6

JUDGING BY THE TIME DEBS and I left the office, I must have flown home. My suitcase was already open and filled on the bed in my guest room. For the past few weeks, I had packed items as I thought about them. It wouldn't be easy to fall asleep at this rate, but who needed sleep when there was this whole other land to conquer across the pond? I checked and rechecked I had my passport. The pictures of the USA that made up an American passport sure were pretty, and soon I'd have my first foreign stamp from an authentic Dublin customs agent. I hardly recognized the sullen woman in the photograph compared to the cheerful person I had become. I'd hardly thought about Faith; that alone was a blessing. In fact, as I thought about downtime in the UK, I grew more determined to add British birds to my lifetime tick-list.

Bird-watching was a hobby I'd inherited from my paternal grandparents. When they were alive, their interest in plants and animals, especially birds, had bordered on the fanatical, especially Grandpa. Many happy days were spent searching for some rare bird along scenic paths all over New York, New Jersey, Connecticut and Pennsylvania, long before

I met Faith. With renewed vigor, I vowed to pick up where I had left off.

The house phone rang. I answered on the first ring.

"I'm so ready," Debs said, her voice at least an octave higher. "You?"

"Absolutely. Let's go through the checklist."

"Okay, I'm glad Marcus sent all the bulky pamphlets and other stuff via airmail. I forgot to mention that I checked with guest services, and they received it all, thank God. I have my flash drives, backup CDs and a master copy of the really important printouts," Debs said.

"Me too. It's all backed up on my computer, e-reader, tablet and phone." I glanced over again to be sure everything was where it should be.

"Overkill, but good thinking," Debs said.

"I'm packed."

"So am I." Debs took a deep breath and let it out slowly. I was tempted to do likewise. "Here goes," she said. "Besides formal wear, dresses, suits, and all that, are you sure you have ample sightseeing attire?" Leave it to Debs to worry about the leisure portions of our trip.

"Check," I said as I fingered through the items in my suitcase, being careful not to mess up my neat packing job.

"Running shoes, decent sport socks, Band-Aids?"

"Check."

"Good. Shorts? Bras, underpants, socks, pantyhose, toothbrush, paste, soap, a raincoat—?"

"I know how to pack. What are you, my mother?"

She laughed. "Heaven forbid. Okay, but one last and most important thought: be prepared, 'cause you never know when a fuckable babe might fall right in your lap. Make sure you have every single necessity for super-duper sex. Now *that's* not something your mother would say, would she?"

"Goodnight, Debs," was all I said.

"Night, night."

My cheeks felt flushed. I had not been in the meat market for so long, I'd passed my sell-by-date. But just in case, as an afterthought, I packed my brand-new and barely used "pussy pouch" that housed condoms, lube, and a vibrator, turning an even brighter shade of pink as I thought about Debs's remark.

Snapping a rubber glove before shoving it into the bag prickled my flesh in a most pleasing way, thinking about the kinkier stuff I used to enjoy with Faith. I packed the pouch and gloves into the suitcase between clothes and prayed my case wouldn't be chosen for inspection. I zipped it shut, wheeled it by the door, and was more than good to go.

Tomorrow seemed like a lifetime away as I crawled into bed. I couldn't remember the last time I was this animated. I drifted off to sleep dreaming of English pubs, Eliza Doolittle, and my mom singing along to "My Fair Lady" during my youth.

I woke before the alarm clock, did a few last-minute chores, and made sure all the appliances were unplugged. The taps weren't leaking, the toilet wasn't running and the lights were all off. I had stopped my mail days before and had given my plants to a neighbor who didn't mind watering them, and at this point, I couldn't think of anything else to do. So I called my parents to say good-bye—again. A glutton for punishment, I listened while my mother made sure I knew everything there was to know about staying safe and being careful.

I stopped her mid-sentence. "Mom, staying safe and being careful are virtually the same."

"I know that, darling," she said, "but you can never be too careful—"

"Or safe," I interrupted.

"Exactly," she said. "You'll be in a strange country. Make sure you know where you're going at all times, and be aware of your surroundings. Don't get lost. No daydreaming."

"They speak English in England," I said pointedly. "And I doubt I'll venture too far from the convention center. If I do, I'll be with Debs or on a guided tour." Daydreaming? I hadn't done that since grade school.

"Good girl. Wait, Dad wants to say something." She put him on the phone.

"Hi honey. Have fun and be sure to say 'blimey,' 'quite right,' and 'cheerio,'" he joked.

"Okay, Dad. Will do."

Mom must have leaned in even closer to the mouthpiece, knowing her, but she raised her voice anyway. "We love you. Don't forget to text as soon as you land, and call once you get your English phone."

"Love you both. Be good, and send hugs to the gang for me."

"Your brothers are already jealous. Baby sister is going to Europe."

"Don't rub it in, or I'll have a huge price to pay when I get back. Just tell them I'll bring home souvenirs. Lots."

"We will. Shoot us e-mails every now and then. Don't forget."

"Stay well. And Dad, don't forget your water pill."

"Janalyn, you just worry about yourself. Make sure you—"

"I know, I know. Love you. Gotta go now. Bye."

I texted Debs, who I knew must be in the airport limo car that was picking us up by now.

On your way? Jx

Almost there. Calm down.

Who says I'm not calm?

I know you. Now chill.

I need a drink.

Soon. After check-in, my treat.

You're a pal. :)

I put my phone back in my bag. Remembered my camera and threw it in there too. The camera on my iPhone was good, but my digital took sharper pictures and was much easier to download.

I couldn't stand the wait. In around seven hours, we would be in Ireland. Add two and a half hours until we landed at Bristol Airport and another two-or-so-hour drive, and we'd be in Devon. I looked up the weather report for Torquay on my phone, then locked up and took the elevator down to the lobby, and just in time too: Debs was waving from the tinted back window of a limousine that had just pulled up.

"Hello there. Is that all you're taking?" she asked as she stepped out. "One suitcase and a carry-on?" She looked dumfounded.

"Yeah, why?"

"Don't look now, but I have two suitcases, a carry-on and my handbag. Are you sure you'll have enough to wear?"

"Are you kidding me? They have laundry service and shopping centers. I am positive I won't be naked, even if I don't do a wash."

Our driver was grumpy for a man who would eventually expect a decent tip, but at least he hefted my suitcase into the trunk.

"What's with Smiley?" I said, nodding toward our driver.

"Beats me, but it may have to do with the weight of my bags."

"What could you possibly need to warrant two cases?"

"I'm prepared for any scenario. How did you fit everything all in one case?"

"I've got talents."

"Yeah, right."

As I settled into the backseat next to Debs, we squeezed hands and bounced around in our seats like schoolgirls.

"I checked earlier." I told her. "Local weather reports show England is enjoying an unusually warm and sunny summer, with very little precipitation expected."

We high-fived, and with it, any hope at sophistication flew right out the open window.

As our limo driver left Manhattan Island for JFK International Airport, he spoke in broken English, thickly accented, that sounded like it came from one of the many countries of Eastern Europe.

"We'll take bridge; tunnel back-up," he grunted.

"Fine, whichever way you think best," Debs said. I let her take the lead.

But as we approached the entrance to the Brooklyn Bridge, my entire body tensed up. I should have insisted on the Midtown tunnel, even if the traffic was lighter on the bridge. Too late. To my disbelief, I started shaking at the sight of it. I shouldn't be so traumatised by something as mundane as the bridge I proposed to Faith on. But I hadn't been near that bridge since that night Faith broke my heart. Debs grasped my hand between both of hers, tightening her grip to steady me. I didn't let go until we were off the bridge and traveling south on the Brooklyn-Queens Expressway. I finally relaxed when I could see the Atlantic Ocean from the car window; the view from Belt Parkway heading east had a calming effect. I managed to tell myself that we were going to have a blast in England.

Luckily the flight was uneventful, a few turbulent spots aside. At one point, it got so bumpy I didn't think a lap belt would provide a strong enough hold. I watched two and a half mediocre movies, ate whatever they put in front of me, and couldn't read more than a sentence or two before my mind wandered. Debs had to pinch me a few times for reassurance we were really flying to Europe.

By the time we landed at Dublin Airport, I was happy to walk the long passages toward to the exit, once I could get my frozen muscles to unthaw and I could walk properly.

"I told you to get up and walk up and down the aisles," Debs scolded, when I kept wobbling.

"I know—next time."

"Are you okay otherwise?"

"Aye, I'm a wee bit tired," I said, imitating the local dialect poorly.

Debs was busy keeping her eyes peeled for exit signs and directions.

I meanwhile, found it hard to walk a straight line, no matter what I had told Debs.

"Are you drunk already?" Debs said, her voice sounding playful and very, very New York in this airport full of lilting Irish accents.

"Aye, high on life."

"Stop saying 'aye'!"

"Aye." I popped a piece of chewing gum into my mouth and offered Debs one, which she accepted. I was grinning while I chewed with my mouth open.

"No cracking, or I'll leave you here to your own defenses," Debs warned while fumbling in her handbag. Between her wheeled carry-on, a leather satchel, and a plastic bag of snacks and magazines she'd purchased after check-in at JFK, I couldn't figure how she could juggle it all.

"What are you looking for?" I asked. "You don't really expect to find anything in there, do you?"

"Our itinerary. Just checking that we have enough time to hit a local bar."

I produced mine out of my breast pocket. "We do. Now let's get us a *proper* Guinness."

We rolled our carry-on luggage, speed-walking on the cool moving sidewalks as we headed outside. My first breath of European air was damp, but I still found it refreshing; it beat recycled airplane air. It wasn't raining, but the fine mist was like walking through a cloud. I spotted a five-star hotel within walking distance. "Let's head over there."

Debs craned her neck in the direction I nodded, "That looks good. Let's."

We stepped into the lobby. "This place looks fancy enough," Debs said. "I'd prefer a traditional Irish pub, but this will do as a second choice. Lead the way."

That's just what I did, and we soon found ourselves at the bar; it wasn't empty. "My treat." I glanced at the menu. "Four euros each? What's that in dollars?"

"Don't worry, I got it," Debs said.

"All right. I'll buy in Torquay, then."

"You got that right."

Debs ordered us a pint each of a proper Guinness, manufactured and sold in Ireland, and we found a nice table and took turns hitting the ladies' room without schlepping luggage.

"Good old Patrick said we should make sure to have a pint or two for him," Debs said as we sat waiting for our drinks. "Come to think of it, I don't remember the last time the poor guy took a vacation that didn't include time off for his coronary bypass."

"You think he would have learned after that major wake-up call," I said. "You know, in Sweden, employees are encouraged to take regular breaks from work, including having an allowance for 'mental health days'. It's greatly improved their job satisfaction, cut down on burnout, and increased people's longevity."

"Yeah, someone needs to remind Marcus, the insufferable slave driver, about that," Debs said with a groan.

Just then, the drinks arrived. We lifted our glasses, examining the dark brew and its thick frothy head, which looked really comforting and smelled delicious.

"Cheers!" Debs said. "To 'mental health days.'"

As we took our first sip, Debs's eyes rolled back into her head. She protected her Guinness brand pint glass with both hands, and I don't think a vice squad could have pried it away from her lips.

When she simply had to take a breath or die, she held the glass in front of her reverently. "It's nothing at all like back home."

I laughed and pointed at where the cream adhered to her top lip. "You have a Guinness mustache."

"You have one too, you know."

An elderly Irish gent at a nearby table leaned over, his ruddy complexion and glassy eyes suggesting he was no stranger to the finer quality of the local brews. "No, lasses, you'll never have a Guinness mustache anywhere but here."

"Good to know." Debs clinked glasses with him, and he ordered us two more pints.

It took what seemed like hours just to pour our drinks. I watched in awe as the bartender first filled a half a pint each, left it there to sit, served more than a few other customers, and then returned to our order to finish up.

The quip opening was so obvious, I couldn't resist: "This long a wait on anything would drive a native New Yorker to drink."

But the wait was well worth it.

I turned to the man. "Thanks again for the drinks. I can't get over how incredible this tastes. You've made two new Guinness fans."

"It's my pleasure to watch you fine-looking ladies enjoy yourselves." He raised his own glass and swallowed a hefty mouthful, wiping his lips with the back of his hand.

Debs drank the second glass of creamy confection much as she did the first, holding the pint glass as if she were hoarding liquid gold. It was that good. Better than any dessert I'd had in a long time.

But all good things had to end.

"Time to go," I told Debs.

"Where are you ladies off to?" the bartender asked.

"We're heading to Devon," I said.

"Devon?" As if a caricature of himself, his lower lip jutted out, forming a comical expression of utter dismay. "What are you going to do a thing like that for? You only just got here."

"We have another flight to catch," I said, taking Debs's suitcase and mine while she put on the layers of clothing she'd peeled off in the bar.

With a wonderful taste in our mouths, a fine feeling in our tummies, and a pleasant buzz, we headed back to the terminal, singing, "My bonnie lies over the ocean," or something to that effect. Mostly laughing was more the way it sounded. We held our boarding passes inserted in our passports ready for the security staff and worked on snapping out of our tipsiness before heading to the departure gate. At that point, my overtired eyes stung so badly, it hurt to blink.

Debs and I breezed through The UK Border Agency at Dublin, well almost. I'm sure we made quite the impression with our over-the-top American jubilation, gushing about Guinness, about the friendly people and amazing greenery, and about how we wished we had longer to really explore. A virtually empty airport didn't help us blend in either. The time difference, five hours ahead of our New York internal clocks, had me almost sleeping on my feet.

I thought the immigration officer, a handsome man in his early thirties, if that, would suck Debs into his booth, ravish her into a coma, and make her his love slave. I stood behind the white line and saw the look in that man's eyes that meant he could see his unborn children as he fell victim to Debs's charm. He seemed to struggle to tear his attention away from her face and back to stamping her passport. It didn't help that she could be the biggest flirt on the planet. It was ages before he said "next" and she was through.

When she was close enough that I could grasp her elbow, I ushered her through pre-boarding check-in. "Sheesh, you could have been knocked up in one of those booths," I cracked.

"No way, he was really sweet. A total gentleman."

I rolled my eyes. "And you could read his character in two minutes—good one. Come on, they still need to check our bags for explosives. Although, I'd say *you're* the bomb."

Debs swatted my arm, and I laughed.

The short flight from Dublin to Bristol was noisy but quick. Debs could barely manage all her luggage, so we rented a cart after we grabbed our suitcases off the conveyor belt. I was already impressed at how efficiently everything was going. We took a plush airport car service straight to the hotel. It was a good thing all costs were on the company bankroll, that's all I can say.

During the one-and-a-half-hour drive, whenever I could get a word in, I talked to Debs, mostly about the scenery. The green fields of England seemed to go on without end, kind of like the American strip malls on Commercial Boulevard in Fort Lauderdale, where one strip mall resembled every other. In England, green fields, some dotted with sheep, cows or just grass, reminded me of a natural habitat of strip malls. More land here was used for farming than shopping. But while I spoke about the landscape, Debs kept steering the conversation back to what the British men would be like. She kept talking about that ever-so-friendly immigration officer.

When I called her on her obsession with him, she said archly, "You seemed to really enjoy the woman who patted you down in Dublin before the flight to Bristol."

"No way," I protested too loudly. Truth was, she had nice eyes, lovely natural red hair—shame it had been held up in such a tight knot. Her bangs had been swept to one side so as not to obscure a decent view of her green eyes; let her loose, and she'd be a total knockout. While I had done my best not to stare at her, truly I did, especially when her warm hands had felt around the inside of my waistband. Thank God she hadn't gone anywhere near my heated crotch: they would have had to pull the smoke alarm.

This reaction to random strangers was not anything new: Call it hormones or unbidden abstinence, but even watching TV was hazardous these days. Commercials with sexy women had me combusting. Both femmes and butches alike turned me to total mush. I was often reduced to a soaking wet horny teenager at the slightest provocation—a nearly exposed breast or well-shaped butt in tight pants could render me insatiable. I thought women my age were supposed to be over sex; it sure wasn't the case with me. The airline security guard had grazed over my breasts, and if she didn't feel my nipples harden, then it was her loss.

"For someone who denies enjoying a pat down," Debs said, "you sure looked turned on to me. I'm sorry, but your pointy tits gave you away. Am I right or am I right!"

"Of course not. That's stupid. And did it ever cross your mind that it might have been a bit chilly after I removed my jacket?"

"Ha! Then why are you blushing riper than a cherry tomato?"

Unwilling to share erotic images with Debs, even if she'd eat it up and share more than a few of her own trysts with me, I ignored her comment and did an abrupt about-face from my salacious thoughts.

"The grass certainly is greener on this side of the pond," I said.

"No doubt about that," she replied as we passed acres of fields.

As we approached the outskirts of Devon, jet lag hit me in an unexpected instant. One minute I was taking it all in, and the next I would be out for the count if allowed the luxury. I powered down the window, hoping fresh air would keep me from dropping off to sleep before we made it to the hotel room. When that didn't help, Debs nudged me each time I started to drift off. Although I thought, *quit waking me up,* loud and clear, reminiscent of all those gentle and not-so-gentle tugs my mother employed to rouse me out of bed for school, I was physically too exhausted to shake her off. I gradually opened my eyes, unable to glare at Debs through the feel of sand under heavy lids.

She sat at the edge of her seat, straining the seat belt, but without a worry in the world. "It has a whole different look than our beaches," Debs said. "I can't believe the sand is brick red!"

Sticking my head out of a moving car made me feel like a kid. The scent of sea air triggered the olfactories to hop, skip and jump toward memory lane, which revived me somewhat.

As I pulled my head back in, I said, "Seagulls cawing remind me of home."

"I know what you mean," Debs said. "We spent summers at the Jersey Shore. What did you guys do?"

"Besides drive my mother crazy the minute we were bored?"

"Boredom isn't even in your vocabulary."

"True. I had to be busy every waking moment. If Mom hadn't guilted my brothers into letting me tag along, I'd have been an insufferable brat. Mom would pile us all into the station wagon and drop us off at Jones Beach, and Dad would pick us up on his way home from work. We'd hit the sand running, body surf, tan, or get hopelessly burnt to a crisp. Sometimes we played touch football. I had to keep up or get lost; I chose to keep up."

I glanced out the window at a great view of the sea from the left and lots of shops and restaurants on the right. There were plenty of people wading, a few swimmers, but nowhere near as many as we got at Jones Beach, back in New York.

"If you think the ocean is cold at Long Island beaches, I hear the water temperature here is much worse," I said.

"I'll stick to indoor swimming then. Our hotel has two pools, indoor and out, a spa and workout room. If we get up early enough, we should go."

Our driver pointed out landmarks. "On the right is Princess Theater, there might be tickets left. And there is the hundred-year-old Torquay Pavilion. It's closed for renovations at the minute, but hopefully the Council will get it sorted before too long. It'd be a shame if they don't reopen it."

"Oh, Janalyn, isn't this beautiful? Look at the fountain over there on the grass. It's like a botanical garden."

I opened the abridged guide I'd bought before I left. "It says here the Torquay Pavilion was built in 1912 as a 'palace of pleasure' to hold concerts and other events."

"I like the sound of that," Debs said.

I grinned. "Why am I not surprised?"

"You can stroll along the pier or stay on the pavement," said our driver. "Just be mindful of traffic, careful not to look the wrong way when using the crosswalk. Those zigzag lines on the road are zebra crossings." He pronounced it *zeh-bra*.

"You have zebras in Torquay?" Debs's eyes widened.

He chuckled. "No, it's what they're called. We have pelican and toucan crossings."

"That's funny. Any other animal crossings we should know about?" I said.

"No, that's it. What I meant to say is pedestrians have right of way, but don't trust without looking first."

I was about to inform him that I'd learned to cross the street as a child and could certainly handle it without lessons, but Debs distracted me before I could comment. "Look over there, Janalyn."

Long and circular rows of lovely flowers were arranged in elaborate displays of color mapped out for optimal visual appeal—primrose, violas, geraniums, marigolds and others; I couldn't keep track. Groups of what looked a lot like foreign students hung out on well-manicured lawns. Tour buses and local ones were buzzing around roundabouts as if they were toys on a play track. There were sunbathers, dog-walkers, shoppers...

Torquay was crammed full of people. Some were using their phones to snap photos of the elaborate adornments that went a long way to further beautify a seaside town—as if the sand and sea weren't enough. As we passed the harbor, every outside table was filled with diners overlooking the bay while enjoying food and drink under the sun. I couldn't wait to explore it all for myself.

Our hotel then appeared before our eyes. The impressive building, dating back to the reign of Queen Victoria, appeared even more majestic situated at the top of a cliff.

"The Imperial Hotel, ladies," our driver said as he cut the ignition. "I'll open the boot." He popped the trunk, thankfully, or else I would not have known why anyone would open a boot, especially when wearing regular shoes. I paid the fare from company funds, tipping twenty percent, as I would a helpful and pleasant New York City cabbie. The man's eyes lit up as if I'd given him a Queen's ransom. He put a hustle in his bustle and insisted on carrying our bags. "Leave everything to me," he said.

I gathered Debs was tired, or else she would have provided constant commentary.

At first glimpse of The Imperial Hotel, all seemed okay.

"The building is nineteenth-century Victorian from Torquay's Golden Age," I told Debs, remembering lines from my guidebook. "Emperor Napoleon III, among other notable celebrities, slept here."

"Interesting." Debs stifled a yawn. I bumped her with my hip.

She grinned sleepily. "I'm listening. Don't take it personally."

"You think we'll have a room with a view?"

"Doubt it."

The driver left us with our bags and a "Cheers" before he left.

I was standing in a hotel that dated back to 1866. The oldest hotel I was familiar with, The Plaza Hotel in New York City, had opened its doors in 1907. Torbay had been a popular seaside resort town that had gone from being a small fishing village of 800 people to a fashionable watering place in Napoleon's day, where the invading French navel fleets had anchored themselves. The naval officers must have liked the sheltered bay so much that they brought their wives with them. There were lots of local celebrities who had lived here too, like Rudyard Kipling, Oscar Wilde, and Elizabeth Barrett Browning, who had benefited from water treatments at a bath house for her medical condition.

The lobby was plush. Everything about this historic hotel reeked of opulence, grandeur, and a timelessness that had not been lost even after what must have been many repairs over the years. It's no wonder that Agatha Christie, a local resident, set a few of her murder mysteries here. It must have been really something in its day. With a perfect view of the ocean, the Imperial was in walking distance to the beaches, the railroad, and High Street, with plenty of tourist attractions, restaurants, and shopping.

There was already a long line at check-in. A hostess with a blonde bob and a mouth full of crooked but perfectly charming teeth welcomed us, clipboard in her hand.

"Good afternoon, ladies. May I take your names, please?"

I spoke for us, and she put a check by our names.

"Welcome. If you'll join the queue for registration, sign in again."

I loved the way she said 'a-*gain*.'

"You'll be given your packets," she continued. "After you've gathered conference materials, be sure to pick up

luncheon tickets for the duration of your stay. Would you
like a cup of tea and a biscuit while you wait?"

"No thanks," Debs said.

I didn't want anything either, as I was still full from the
Guinness. Once out of earshot, Debs leaned into me and
whispered, "How quaint. She sounds so English. I love it."

"We *are* in England."

"Thank you for stating the obvious."

"You're welcome, my dear."

We weren't standing around long before we heard
a raucous laugh. Debs beat me to it and nodded in the
direction of the commotion.

"Look over there. Who is she?"

I turned to see where Debs pointed and fixated on the
friendly little group, especially the center of attention: She
was nearly a head taller than the other women, but that's not
the only reason she stood out from the crowd. For all eyes
were riveted on this one woman, including mine and Debs's.

She was well built—I want to say sturdy—with messy
short hair and dressed in muddy cargo shorts. In fact, her
ankle boots and socks were caked with mud, as if she had
just come from a hike, and I was hard-pressed to find a part
of her not at least smudged in dirt, if not outright covered in
it. This was certainly not the attire for conference attendees
anyone would expect. But the most distinguishing feature
in this most unusual ensemble was the bloodied gauze that
encased her left hand.

"I wonder what that's all about?" Debs asked.

"Maybe she's homeless," I said, "and had to fight off a
group of muggers or nasty savages."

"She can't be homeless. They just handed her a course
packet and nametag."

"Oh right, can you read it?"

"No."

My gaze remained fixed on the not-homeless stranger, but I hadn't ruled out 'mud wrestler' as a means of explaining her appearance. She and the organizer seemed like old friends as she spoke with grand gestures and an animated expression to the entire attentive group. It was hardly the rapport one would expect between a derelict and the chief of the conference. Upon closer inspection, I was immediately taken by her commanding presence. She was surrounded by people who appeared to hang on her every word. I didn't want to turn away, but the pesky problem was that it was our turn at the registration table. I had no choice.

Debs and I made our way to the desk to find our names and were greeted politely.

"*Hallo*. Welcome to Devon and The Imperial Hotel," said the woman manning the table. She explained a few things in our packets. "Some parts of the conference will take place at the Riviera Conference Centre, but you'll have plenty of warning, and transportation is provided, if you don't want to take the short walk; but enough of that after your long journey. Do get all settled, and don't hesitate to ask any questions you might have. Have a good conference, ladies. And again, welcome."

After we were all set, the small group, including the apparent mud wrestler had vanished. I had this sudden urge to comb the venue for the intriguing woman.

Debs had other things on her mind. "We're just in time for afternoon tea," she said. "Shouldn't we freshen up first?"

"Yes, let's dump our stuff. Are you really okay we're sharing?"

"Yes, of course. Marcus gave us a limit on the expense account. Wouldn't you rather use it to hit the night life?"

"I suppose," I said. But what I did want to do was take excursions to the moors, Kents Caverns, Brixham, Paignton, and whatever else we could fit in with an already-bursting schedule. Right now, though, it didn't take long for jetlag to set in like concrete, making movement nearly impossible.

Our room upstairs was so luxurious, Debs truly could have no problem sharing with me. But it's not like I could really appreciate it with the waves of exhaustion rolling over me. "I can't keep my eyes open another second. Feel free to grab tea without me." I yawned.

"Okay, if you're sure?" Debs said, primping herself in the bathroom mirror.

"I am."

"It says here that the formal icebreaker is at seven o'clock tomorrow evening, but they're having afternoon tea later. Should I come back and get you?"

"Nah, I will be down before that, but thanks." The last sound I heard was the clicking of the door as it closed behind Debs.

I must have been in a deeply sleep-deprived state, because when I awoke, I remembered bits and pieces of my ridiculous dream: The mystery woman from registration was in it, wearing her mud-encrusted shorts and boots like a badge. She then became the mud wrestler in an arena. Avoiding the bandaged hand, she single-handedly fought off muddy lions, which in reality inhabit grasslands, open woodlands and scrub country. If they happen to traipse through mud, they are forever licking themselves clean. But in my dream, this mud wrestler defended her human pride—made up of the conference organizer and a few other delegates I had seen earlier. In the quite preposterous way dreams often have, she fought off lions as muddied as pigs after a good wallow, and she did this all with one bare hand. Meanwhile we all scrambled to find where the first meeting was to be held now that the lions, tigers and bears were occupying our seats. The annoying dream had me chasing my own tail, searching for an empty room but getting knee-deep in mud. I woke with a start, instantly relieved it was only a dream.

I spent the rest of the night in exhausted, dreamless sleep. It wasn't until the next morning that I regretted missing afternoon tea, but being refreshed and ready to give my full attention at the convention was a necessary trade-off.

Chapter 7

THE VIEW FROM OUR FOURTH-FLOOR room the next morning was amazing. Debs had the doors to the balcony wide open, lending a vacation feel to the space as the cool ocean breeze brushed past us. It went against the natural order of things to be zipping up a skirt instead of stepping into a bathing suit.

"I'm glad we had opted to share a nicer room with a sea view."

"I'll say. Will you look at that?" Debs held onto the balcony railing on tiptoes. "I can see inside the penguin center."

"What penguin center?"

"The sea aquarium." She came back inside, lifted a bunch of pamphlets off the table, and flipped through them until she found the one she wanted. "It's called Living Coasts—Torquay's Coastal Zoo and Aquarium. And they're in walking distance. Cool."

"Nice." I tucked in my blouse. "You can't tear yourself away from that view can you?"

"No way. Although I can't wait to get started, it's a shame we have to work today. The water looks so inviting, and the penguins are so cute. I could just stand here all day. That's a funny-looking gull. Oh, and there's more than one."

"Let me take a gander." I had no idea what she was talking about. All the seagulls looked ordinary to me. "Where?"

"You silly goose." It was never a good idea to get into a pun war with Debs. She always won. "Look there." She pointed out the window. "Flying around inside the net. The gulls with the handlebar moustaches."

"Those are not gulls. I'm not a hundred percent sure—I'd guess they're Terns, maybe, but wait a minute." I opened my bird book and found the section I was searching. "They're definitely Terns, but this book doesn't have the exact species. I'll Google it later." Grandpa would be so proud I named the group correctly, I thought. Was it an omen that we lucked out with this room? Maybe I would resume birding after all. After Faith, I hadn't had interest in anything other than my job and working out. It was about time I found a relaxing hobby to balance out my life.

I called out to Debs, who had pulled herself away from the window only to plant herself in front of the mirror. "Are you ready? I don't want to miss Dr. Wright's talk. I've read her articles, and I hear she has a book coming out soon. And today's topic is controversial. It should be interesting to get her take on the changes in the food industry and how unorthodox production methods have affected the population."

Debs easily slipped into debate mode. "It would be great if we could grow and process our own food and have enough to feed every person on the planet, but let's be practical."

"Exactly. Can we please go now?"

"Yep, ready to roll. Do I look okay?"

"Perfect." I had the handy-dandy backpack they gave out at registration; it had plenty of room for everything: a laptop, leaflets, pads, you name it.

Stepping into my heels, I briefly checked myself in the mirror.

"You should wear skirts more often," she remarked. "You have great legs. Although those shoes can hardly be considered heels, Janalyn; they're so lame."

"Gee, thanks." My sarcasm was unmistakable. "If I wear the higher heels in the name of fashion, that's exactly what I'll be—lame! Well, I have sneakers in my bag. I'll put them on instead."

"You wouldn't!"

"Want to bet?"

Debs shook her head in that disapproving way. I was tempted to keep on the low-heeled pumps I'd paid a small fortune for in the vain pursuit of comfort, just to show her I meant business. But first impressions took precedence, and in a summer suit, silk blouse, and the dreaded heels that pinched my toes, I knew I would fit right in with the other conference members.

"You win. Let's go."

We left the room and headed to the elevator. The hallway maintained a Mediterranean-style Victorian aura—from the ornate moldings, sconces and wallpaper down to the carpet. I could imagine passing Agatha Christie along the way, especially after noticing a plaque with her likeness on the wall by reception. The elevator ride was silent, but the moment the doors opened, a room-filled with the buzz of chatter filled the air. Debs and I weaved around but soon split up.

I grabbed the last two seats in the large meeting room while Debs went in search of caffeine. Once she had returned, I surveyed the room as I sipped the steaming brew she had brought me. I checked that my name badge was affixed onto the lapel of my jacket just as the organizer, a Rachel Smith, came over to personally welcome us.

"Hello, Miss Jacobs. Miss Foster-Baker?" she said. "That's a mouthful."

Debs smiled at her. "'Debs is just fine," she said. "It's so nice to meet you. May I call you 'Rachel'?"

"Of course. Thank you both for coming. I hope your travels from America were pleasant?" She sounded posh, but without the airs. "I've never been, but I've always wanted to."

Debs and I smiled.

"What's wonderful is being here in Devon—we've never been," Debs said.

"It's a pretty part of the country," Rachel said. "I hope you'll get a chance to sample some of it. If there's anything you need, don't hesitate to ask." Her voice turned bright. "Oh, I see we'd better get started. I have the honor of introducing today's speaker, Dr. Wright—a local celebrity. Having the con here in Devon was her idea. I'll see you around ladies."

"Did *you* know we had a celeb in our midst?" I said after Rachel walked away.

"I've heard the name, but hadn't realized she was famous. Do you know anything about her?"

"Nothing more than reading her work. She makes many valid points, but can she, or anyone, invoke worthwhile changes? The food industry has a powerful lobby. I doubt the likes of Wright or any of us will have that great an impact."

I vaguely remembered seeing a stamp-sized photo of Dr. Wright but couldn't remember many details, so I looked up at the podium in curiosity. Rachel Smith introduced her, and when our speaker took the stand, I nearly fell out of my chair.

"That's the mud wrestler," I whispered to Debs.

"Who?"

"You know, the one caked in mud who we originally thought was a homeless stranger."

"Oh, yeah. You're right. She sure cleans up well."

I'll say. I couldn't take enough of her in. Standing taller than her presenter, she raised the microphone to level with her lips, painted a subtle shade of red. Her subtle makeup, if she was wearing anything other than lightly tinted lipstick, lent credibility to her face by downplaying her sexy lips. While she wasn't dressed any sharper than the rest of us, in her tailored multi-colored pin-striped blouse and body-hugging taupe slacks, this woman easily stood out in a crowd with her inherent star quality. Her neatly coiffed hairdo, a stylish feathery cut in varying shades of gold with every hair in place, looked like she'd just stepped out of a salon. Gone were the smudges of dirt and the sweat streaking her face. All cleaned up, her complexion was clear with a youthful glow, just beyond pale and not quite tanned. Her eyes, well, her eyes were blue, bright, and for lack of a better word, beautiful.

"Thank you for the generous introduction, Rachel, well done," Wright said. "Now, what do you want in return?"

Rachel Smith put her hand up and laughed, shaking her head. "Endless favors."

Dr. Wright paused and waited for the laughter to die down. "Welcome, everyone, to the First Annual Wellness at Work and World Health Initiative. We have an impressive roster of attendees with two-hundred and fifty delegates from all over the world. I'm honored to be here among many great minds in various fields from medicine, nutrition, food technology, economics, you name it. My personal thanks to every member of this committee, particularly..." She rattled off many names, some I knew and some I had never heard before.

Her voice was resonant, but what impressed me most was that she didn't rely on the usual quirks of public speaking, like, *um*, *er*, or some annoying pet saying, my least favorite at the moment being 'the reality is.' It was a pleasure to listen to someone who had command of the English language.

"According the World Health Organization, 'Health is a state of complete physical, mental, and social well-being and not merely an absence of disease or infirmity.' We are privileged to have members of WHO among us. Will the following delegates please stand when I call your name?"

My attention honed in on her accent. She could have spoken gibberish, and I would have hung on her every word.

"We also have representatives from The Bureau of Labor Statistics and The Centers for Disease Control and Prevention. Don't be afraid to enlist their help. Don't be too proud to beg." That gained a laugh from the audience.

"There's been a global shift in the healthcare paradigm, moving from traditional medical practice, treating illness as it arises, toward prevention-focused strategies. It's what we've been promoting all along, but now governments faced with a healthcare crisis—and on a level more close to home, employers who face huge prices paying out sick leave—we need a societal and community outreach plan to reduce chronic illness. In 2002, the Institute of Medicine called on both the corporate and public health communities to join forces in promoting health and prevention efforts through collaboration and research. Have you all heard of the *Ottawa Charter*? It was the first international conference on health promotion way back in the mid-1980s. You'd think in all that time we would have a handle on this problem, but instead we're seeing an exponential increase in the numbers of chronic illness."

She spoke for an hour and conducted a question-and-answer period that went on for thirty or more minutes. Yet the morning flew. After she stepped off the podium, we were granted a break, and immediately, she was surrounded by a flock of attendees all vying for her undivided attention. Debs and I checked out our schedules and headed to a nutrition overview given by a registered dietitian nutritionist, also from America. Afterwards, Debs and I headed to the lunch buffet.

"The dietitian was very good. She touched upon many important topics, but as a public speaker she doesn't have the star quality of Dr. Wright. Now *she's* an amazing speaker," Debs said.

"Dr. Wright is one tough act to follow." I perused the buffet table for the beginning of the line. And under my breath, I mumbled, "No doubt about that."

"Let's see what's for lunch." Debs was eyeing the menu selection as listed on the free-standing easel by the tableware. I took two trays and handed one to Debs. We helped ourselves to silverware, dinner rolls and salad.

Once seated, we introduced ourselves to everyone. I couldn't pronounce some of the foreign names, but I probably would not have remembered them even if I could.

"This steak and kidney pie tastes delicious. But what are these meatball looking things?" I asked.

Debs shrugged. I called over the nearest server.

"Excuse me, what are these?"

"Faggots in a rich sauce," she said, in a thick Polish accent.

"Excuse me?"

"It's a traditional dish in the UK."

I made a point of not curling up my lips with distaste. "What's it made of?"

"I'll ask chef. Be back in a minute."

After she walked away, I asked Debs, "Now why would I want to eat a faggot in rich sauce?"

Debs laughed. "Beats me."

True to her word, the server was soon back at our table. "It's pig heart and liver with bacon and crumbs of bread."

"Thank you, I think." I was happier not knowing and placed my helping on Debs's plate.

"Oh, no you don't. You took it, you eat it."

"You're not my mother."

"Good thing for that."

"I'm ready for dessert. Want some?"

"No thanks, you go, though. I want to hit the little girl's room. Meet you at the next meeting. Whoever gets there first saves us a seat."

"You got it." I ambled over to the "pudding" section, expecting chocolate, rice, or tapioca pudding, only to find wide assortments of cakes in finger-sized portions. I took about five of them. When I noticed how the British attendees liberally poured hot custard from heavy-duty insulated white jugs over their Victoria sponge, I did too. So much for making healthy choices. I then selected a meager helping of fresh berries in four varieties so I wouldn't be completely without redemption.

We were well into the afternoon session before my head stopped spinning with all I planned to learn and accomplish. I'd worked so hard to get here and, so far, so good. It was surreal to finally be among peers from other nations, and if surveyed to comment on what I thought of the convention, my report would be glowing. But like most conferences I'd attended, there were amazing and not-so-great presenters. Not all people were born lecturers. It was a shame that the afternoon presenter had the personality of a sloth after such a dynamic speaker like Dr. Wright and even the dietitian, who had entertained us with her funny anecdotes. Not only was postprandial tiredness from such a heavy lunch setting in, but we were forced to sit for over an hour that felt like forever. His pompous prattle droned us all to sleep. My mind unavoidably wandered astray, landing a few rows ahead on an intriguing butch. I swore I could feel my pupils immediately dilate as I realized it was Dr. Wright.

She sat tall. I hoped she'd turn around and grant me another view of her face. From the way she was positioned in her seat, legs spread wide, it was like she owned the space. Her briefcase was by her side on the floor. I got a glimpse of her profile as she bent down to open her bag and removed a small black carrying case. She glanced in the direction of the time keeper at the back—he held up a sign saying *five minutes left,* and then she extracted what looked like fancy-schmancy binoculars, placing the cord around her neck and adjusting the collar of her shirt. I couldn't imagine why she'd need binoculars, but imagined that she might be a bird lover like me; that would be interesting.

A handsome, long-legged, ample-breasted Brit would be a nice souvenir, if I was looking for that sort of thing. It was nearing the end of the session, and I was itching to make a hasty getaway or maybe to accidentally-on-purpose bump into her. I'd have to figure out what to say, but it would be a start. We had fifteen minutes between sessions. As it turned out, when they dismissed us at the end of the talk, the hallway was too narrow for the amount of traffic pushing through it. I couldn't get close enough, but I kept my eye on her when I could.

On the way to the current lecture, she walked into the Gold Room just ahead of me. It was hard to miss my first close-up glimpse of her fantastic tush as I made small talk with a man from Belgium. Unexpectedly, she turned around to converse with someone who had tapped her shoulder. Despite being engaged in conversation with someone else, I was quite certain she glanced my way more than once. I personally could not stop staring. My stomach was doing flip-flops like I was some horny teen who was sure she had spotted her true love at long last. Her milky complexion, light eyes, pronounced cheekbones and tapered jaw made an instant impression on me. I was close enough to notice her irises, bordering on liquid blue, which brightened significantly when she smiled. I wished I had been closer and pushed my way in to sit next to her, but I had hesitated too long, and the seats on either side were promptly taken.

What idiot misses an opportunity like that? Yours truly, that's who. I consoled myself with the fact that although she fit the criteria on my rusty gay radar, that did not guarantee she was a lesbian. I'd have to get to know her first.

It was a long afternoon. The moment the boring speaker announced a break, I rushed toward refreshments. Dr. Wright arrived first. I made double sure I was right by her side. True American style, I blurted the first thing that came to mind.

"Could this guy be any duller?" I bit my tongue. What if he was a friend of hers? Or worse, what if she thought I wasn't overjoyed to be here?

She turned, peered quite intently into my eyes, and with a bemused smile, replied, "He's an arrogant prat. His articles boast of bloody useless data; I chuck them in the bin straight away. He wants sacking, but the bigwigs are soft." On the podium, she sounded posh, but on a personal level, she was actually down-to-earth and quite relaxed in her choice of words.

"Sacking, as in potatoes?" I asked.

"You're joking? No, sacking as in fired."

She helped herself to coffee and a jelly donut.

"Where are the tea and crumpets?" I asked.

She raised an eyebrow. "Tea is over there, and I'm sure you can get a crumpet if you ask."

"That's okay, there's plenty to nosh on here."

"Nosh? Are you from New York or something?"

"Yes, actually, I am."

Rachel Smith walked over. "I ate so much for lunch," she told Dr. Wright, "that it will be near impossible to find room for any of these lovely nibbly bits."

"Sure you can," Dr. Wright assured her.

"Well, if you insist." Rachel placed a cake on her plate and scampered off to mingle.

Nibbly bits? That's a funny expression, but I immediately zoomed in on Dr. Wright's mouth and longed to nibble on those nibbly bits, along with other delectable parts, until a scone and cream caught my eye. Catering even provided small jars of authentic strawberry jam rather than artificially colored and flavored red jelly packets that could double as table sugar. I dropped a scone on my plate, sliced it open, and then proceeded to cover it generously with the cream and jam. I put it aside just long enough to pour tea and a bit of milk into my cup—a lovely cup and matching saucer my grandmother would approve—and filled both hands with the takings. I followed her over to an empty free-standing table.

One bite, and bliss exploded in my mouth. This was more like it. I sipped the perfectly brewed beverage. The tea tasted much better in England, I decided. I looked up to find Dr. Wright's gaze transfixed somewhere around my lips. Unable to quench my sudden desire, I stared right back at her, totally besotted. With her head slightly tilted, Dr. Wright raised her eyebrows and shot me a flirtatious smile that blew me away. She was so damn hot, it was amazing I didn't boil over at the mere sight of her. I dabbed the corner of my lip with my tongue out of habit.

"We have 'prats' in America too," I said, not entirely sure what 'prat' meant, but I figured it wasn't a compliment. "Do you suppose this delicious tea will be strong enough for the jolt I'm after?"

"I doubt it." She held up her donut. "That's why I'm eating rubbish and drinking coffee. I see you chose the scone."

Despite going back on the promise I had made to myself that the Victoria Sponge and custard was the last treat of the day, I stuck my finger into the decadent cream for another taste—you know, just to be *sure* I really liked it.

"Oh, yummy. Too yummy for a health professional whose main goal is to guide the public toward improved eating habits, but whatever." I was fully aware that I was indulging in a sugary, fat-laden dessert and relishing the delightful feel in my mouth as a substitute for other sensual delights—namely having sex with the woman who openly watched me enjoy my cream like a voyeur in heat. What a flirt!

"You like clotted cream then?" she said, her eyebrow quirked.

"I love it, but did you just say 'clotted'? Why clotted?"

"They use the milk from Jersey or Guernsey cows because it's higher in fat than milk from other cows."

"Oh God, now you tell me! So much for being a minor indulgence—this is major. How do they clot the cream?"

"My granny used to make it. She would pour the milk into shallow pans and leave it out for about twelve hours until the cream rose to the top. Then she'd heat it close to the boil until the surface began to wrinkle. She would then refrigerate it, and when it was ready she'd scoop up the clotted cream."

"It sounds like a lot of work."

"Blimey," she said. "I haven't had a Devon cream tea since I was little. It was a special treat. You can't come to Devon without having one."

"You've got a point." I gathered another dollop. "Would you like to share some of mine...to, uh, refresh your memory?"

"It's a bit rich, but all right then; go on." Her plump red lips parted in preparation, and my mouth went dry as moisture collected in my pants. I couldn't take another bite of the scone, slathered as it was with that clotted cream, but I sure could live vicariously watching her devour it.

She didn't have a free hand and made no move to put down her plate or the cup and saucer despite having a table at her disposal. Could this have been a calculated move on her part? I suspected the answer was yes. I did the only thing I could. I brought the treat toward her waiting lips. Her heated breath made the cream slide off the piece of scone onto my thumb and forefinger. Without pausing, she lapped it up, licking my fingers as she did, which caused a delightful twinge below. After the cream was gone, she lingered before slowly pulling away. One more second and I would have begged for her mouth to take me too. Her eyes practically rolled back in her head as she swallowed, amidst moans of gastronomic pleasure. I shared her bliss but in a totally different way. Still, in that moment, I felt this unbelievable connection.

I immediately dismissed it since there was no way on earth I was going to fall for a woman on the other side of the pond. No way in hell either!

She took a tiny step back and intently gazed into my eyes. With her thumbs hooked into her belt loops, standing tall, yet at ease, she looked so sexy. It's no wonder I averted my attention to her hands. But that didn't exactly help: such capable hands, and resting oh-so-close to her crotch, tapping fingertips near her zipper. I slurped my tea, happy it had cooled some, or I would have scalded my tongue.

"There's only one other cream I enjoy more." Her voice deepened as she hinted at hidden meanings. The wider she grinned, the redder my face grew. I tried to ignore the aphrodisiac effect she had on me, as my radar pinged with delight.

"It's stuffy in here," she said. "Want to get some fresh air?"

"I'd love to."

I should have said, "No thanks" instead. Her vibes caused every caution signal to practically blare in my ears and blind me with flashing lights. She was coming on too fast.

I hadn't dated in five years, much less spoken to other women besides my colleagues, so how was I supposed to proceed once we got outside? I didn't want to lead her on, but I did want to get to know her. What was the protocol for showing interest in a British woman? Was it the same as for an American? Did they have different rules? I followed her blindly.

She led me to a patio overlooking the water. I was acutely aware of her hand against the small of my back, a gesture that hinted chivalry was not dead. There was a tanker not far from shore and a ferry en-route to the peninsula in the distance. It was a clear day. I could see the breakwater and the lighthouse, as well as pedestrians and their dogs. She chose a table, held my chair, and sat down in the one beside me. Was this a typical English gesture? I doubted it. I could have sorely used a book on British social norms.

"Thank you, this is lovely," I said. "I noticed your binoculars; they look top-of-the-line."

"They are actually quite good. I got them on offer at eBay."

"You must be serious about birding then?"

"I am. What about you? Have you seen any interesting wild American birds?"

"A whooping crane, once."

"That's brilliant." She stroked my arm. "Look there." With a gentle hand she guided my shoulder until I faced the right direction. "See the Cormorant there?"

"Oh, yes, I almost missed him. Thanks." I absently patted her thigh in appreciation. When her muscles flexed beneath my touch, I withdrew my hand, hoping she didn't read my touch as encouragement. I wasn't sure I was ready to go that route—not yet, at least. A small measure of relief came after others had joined us outdoors.

"Where does that ferry go?" I asked, to keep the conversation going.

"Brixham," she said. "A fishing village. During the Middle Ages, it was the largest fishing port in the southwest. Today it's still one of the largest fishing ports in England. But most people go there to shop, fish off the breakwater, have a meal, or swim in one of the many coves. It's a lovely place. You should try to get over there."

"I hope to do some sightseeing. Thanks." I couldn't help sounding stiff, but I was so flustered about this attractive woman's attention, I couldn't focus on the conversation long enough to come across as what I hoped was approachable and fascinating. I worried she was already bored to tears by my lack of animation, but then the next thing she said shocked the hell out of me.

"Let's sneak out," she said, a devious glint in her eye, when the others were yards ahead of us.

I didn't mean to gape, but this woman could not be serious. To skip out on part of this groundbreaking symposium was totally irresponsible, especially since she was keynote speaker no less. "That's naughty, don't you think?"

"I prefer to live dangerously."

"I can't miss the next afternoon session." I was not about to miss doing everything in my power to ensure the success of this project. I couldn't let my company down, and I certainly wasn't going to let myself or Debs down either. And on a grander scale, if I could be so presumptuous, I was not prepared to let the public that could benefit down either. "I'm sorry, no."

She sighed. Was it a sigh of disappointment or resignation or was she just dismissing me forever more? I hadn't a clue what she was thinking when she finally said, coolly, "No worries. Cheers, then, yeah." She pushed back her chair and stood up. Before I could explain, she had the gall to turn and walk away. I had to close my mouth or catch flies, as they say.

We strolled back inside separately, her in the lead. Although this granted me a nice view of her attractive backside, her abrupt change in attitude wounded my pride. At first this pissed me off, but then I thought about missed opportunities and my anger disappeared. Instead I was overcome with sadness, when I should have been celebrating my dedication to work. It was just like me to mess up what could have been a good thing for my private life. Her butch complimented my femme: God, I had loved it when she had led me outside and placed her hand on the small of my back, too intimate a gesture for new acquaintances, a touch that caused an electrical current all the way down to my toes. I still couldn't get over how she had held my chair and had chosen to sit so close. She was smooth, smart, loved nature and her lips were extremely kissable. We would make a nice couple under other circumstances.

I entered the darkened hall and was temporarily blinded. My eyes took a while to adjust, but I never lost sight of her.

"See you later," I said when I managed to catch up to her, sounding wistful despite efforts to remain aloof. I hated that we had to part. But when I got back to my seat, she was right behind me.

"Hiya, Gwyneth, mind if we switch seats?" Dr. Wright said to a woman who looked as if she'd bite the head off a mouse if Dr. Wright asked her to.

"Sure thing, Dr. Wright. You go ahead."

Things were looking up.

I briefly glanced over at my new neighbor but quickly busied myself in search of...I didn't at first know what. I looked for something, anything, to pull out of my bag of tricks. It might have looked odd, but I ended up with two identical pens. As she wasn't holding a writing implement, I handed her one of mine.

"Thank you," she said.

I then gave her an extra notepad, which she immediately used to write me a note.

I have all the notes from every member of this panel, verbatim, so don't worry if you miss anything. I can share.

Soon we were exchanging notes back and forth, barely managing to stifle giggles as we continued to pass silly notes throughout the next panel. She had lived in Devon all her life and accurately guessed I was from Brooklyn, New York. She had me pegged as a ringer for Fran Drescher, which was close, although Fran Drescher is from Queens, as I informed her. But truth be told, the actress from "The Nanny" and I were from somewhat similar backgrounds, the main similarity being that we are both Jewish; but I don't think

Dr. Wright had thought of that. Although Ms. Drescher and I had brown hair and eyes, same-shaped face and generous mouth, or so I was told, I was a bit taller, less curvy, and I promise, I didn't have the signature Fran Drescher laugh.

I ripped a page out of my notebook and scribbled, *My name's Janalyn. What's yours?* I had read her papers. I couldn't believe I didn't remember her first name. But it was just as well, because it allowed me to look the smooth operator instead of the starstruck groupie. I needed some ammunition given my awe of her celebrity, not to mention the pesky control she had over my awakened libido. I tore my eyes off her bosom to read what she wrote.

ROBIN, it said in block letters, *with an* I.

Was that *I* supposed to be for emphasis or to exert some kind of warning about commanding authority? In response, I drew a childish picture of a Robin redbreast, to which she drew a jar of jam next to *Hiya Jamalyn*. I grinned.

That's JaN-alyn with an N, *not JaM-alyn*, I wrote, now grinning broadly. Drawings turned into more questions, and each question prompted her to run her fingers along my neck. She was a bit forward, but as I sat on the edge of my seat, my body thrummed for more. I didn't miss how she used any opportunity to touch me, to direct my attention.

Robin whispered in my ear, "Ja*nnn*, let's sneak out later. We can network on our own tonight and make up for lost time with the others tomorrow. Nobody will notice, yeah?"

I had been worried she was a player. Now, my suspicions were confirmed.

"Everybody will notice if you're not there," I whispered.

"Rachel will cover for me. Will you do it?"

I hesitated. "I'm supposed to be hobnobbing with people from WHO and exchanging advice with public policy planners from around the world...you know, doing important things, not ditching the first chance I'll have to make myself heard at the icebreaker." There, I'd said it, and quickly, I might add, but it was out there. I couldn't imagine Robin with an *I* didn't feel the same way.

"That's exactly what I'm here to do, but I'll tell you this right now, you won't get within a hair of anyone important tonight. They'll be swarmed with introductions alone, so why waste what could be a great night with me when I can get you a private meeting with anyone you so much as desire?"

"Excuse me? And how do you plan to do that?"

"Simple, I have connections in the World Health Organization and as keynote, well, I could pull a few strings." She sure was full of herself, but that didn't stop me from liking her or wanting to spend time in her presence. If anything, I was flattered she chose to spend time with me.

I had this internal debate going on like my brain and I were candidates in the presidential primaries.

"Can I let you in on a little secret?" She moved close enough for me to feel her heated breath caress my face. It was hard to disguise my tremble.

"What's that?" I asked, not wanting to move back now that she had closed the distance between us.

"Before the Americans, Canadians and Asians came over, the Europeans had a meeting. It was a dress rehearsal of sorts. I can tell you anything you need to know. Missing a couple of hours here or there won't get in the way of accomplishing your goals. All right?"

What could it hurt if I were to skip out now? Who would really miss me at the icebreaker tonight besides Debs, and I knew she'd sooner join a convent than have me miss an opportunity to get to know someone who was eligible and apparently interested. This felt wrong on so many levels, but so right, Dr. Wright, I chuckled to myself. If the keynote speaker could miss a couple of hours, who was I to hold back?

"Lead the way!" I said in a jubilant whisper, like we were in cahoots, "Where shall we go…to, um, *network*?"

"I've been told there are migrant birds just arrived from Africa at Bovey Heathfield. The nightjars come here to procreate," she said.

"Whoa! Nightjarring, I'd love to! I've never seen them in their natural habitat before. Nightjars would be a great tick for my world bird list."

"My car is just outside. We need to get to Bovey before nightfall if we want to spot the nightjars. They're well camouflaged even at dusk, but I think we'll be fine if we leave straight away after tea."

"This gets me all excited," I said in a low voice. "Maybe I'll get lucky."

"Yeah? What else excites you?" Robin looked at me like I was a delicacy she was savoring.

I shot her my most devilish smile. "Wouldn't you like to know?"

I had no idea what game I was playing, but I was diving in head first, and I wasn't sure the pool was deep enough.

Chapter 8

ROBIN DROVE FAST—TOO FAST. SHE had a silver hummingbird hanging from her rearview mirror, which swung like it was really flying. Taking the blind, winding turns on the wrong side of the road at high speeds was jarring enough, but when we arrived in a desolate area, parking in a vacant lot near empty factories, my imagination ran wild.

"Is this safe?" I asked. As the perceived danger quotient rose, surprisingly, so did my libido.

"Completely. Any bloke up to no good wouldn't hang around here on the off chance two women showed up, now would he?" She grinned. "Besides, it's not like we're defenseless."

Before I got out of the car, she handed me my knapsack I had stowed in the 'boot,' which was such a silly name for a trunk! It was almost as bad as saying 'bonnet' for the hood, because in my mind, a bonnet is what Miss Muffet wore on her head while sitting on her tuffet eating her curds and whey. Several times I asked her to spell a word, only to realize it was her pronunciation and not the word itself I didn't know.

"You talk funny," Robin said after this had happened more than a few times. But seriously, who was she kidding?

I hesitated by the car to adjust my binoculars and focused the lenses on a bush. It wasn't quite dark yet, but it would be soon enough. I shivered.

"You're not scared, are you?"

"God no," I lied, watching each step as I followed along the well-worn path, appreciating the mosaic of purple heather and yellow gorse, until we stood at the top of the clearing near a shoulderblade-high granite boulder overlooking the heathland below. We listened intently, taking shallow breaths. All I could hear was what sounded like frogs.

"Euuuuurrrrrruerrrrrr."

"Hear that?" she said.

"Oh yeah...that's what it says in the book. Their call does reverberate."

"You did your homework."

"I enjoy learning about the local inhabitants of whatever area I happen to travel," I said, as if I was this savvy world traveler.

"I do too—especially the local women."

She was a player, I told myself again. But the difference was this time, I didn't even care.

"Oh, really?" I said.

She grasped my hand, and with it, the most pleasant sensations traveled through my body. "Walk this way, I hear them over there."

I let her lead, becoming more aware of her rich lemongrass and sea salt scent. She was so determined and capable in everything she did; even the way she walked was regal. Her knowledge of the surroundings was textbook accurate without sounding boastful. Her deep voice lulled me into an erotic trance.

A male nightjar, with his wings clapping, flew right by us.

"Did you see that?" I said, excitement mounting.

She kissed me then, and I melted in her arms. As I luxuriated in her soft lips, she backed me up to a boulder nearby, and our urgent kisses grew hotter and more fervent. The pebbled pavement littered with twigs and lush prickly vegetation would be inhospitable for a comfy quickie, but lust overshadowed inconvenience, and I began immediately considering how to make it work.

The insistent niggle to my senses raised doubts in my mind. Did I really desire a mad dash to get naked, followed by uninhibited meaningless coupling, only to leave in a week's time with nothing but faded memories? I mean, no matter how good I imagined sex with her would be...

"Wait." I placed my palm on her chest. Her heart beat as wildly as mine. "Incredible," I murmured, distracted.

"I want more," she said, between kisses.

"This is just too fast."

"You are a baby."

I wasn't entirely comfortable with the tone of her voice. Was she just teasing?

"And you're pushy." I moved past her and started to walk back toward the car when the nightjar's courtship dance presented itself a short distance away. I focused my binos and stood awestruck for a moment. Poking my elbow into her arm, I whispered, "Oh my God! Would you look at that?"

We watched in silence until she said, "Well, at least someone is getting a good shagging."

"Maybe if you weren't so impetuous." I was torn between being turned on by someone who obviously asserted her dominance, but I wasn't completely comfortable letting go of this amount of control to another woman. It had been too long, call me cautious, but I was also rusty and didn't want to fuck this up. Why should I care what she thought of me, I wondered, but I did care, a lot, and that's why I stopped her when my body wanted the complete opposite.

"That's a big word, impetuous, that is."

"Hasty then."

"Come on, show's over. I'll drive you back." She seemed impatient more than anything else. Maybe she wasn't used to not getting her own way, and I'd irritated her in some way by not going along with her whim.

Her wonderful ardent mood from moments ago turned black so quickly, it was like a sudden rain cloud had dumped cold water on top of my head. The guilt of thinking I must have led her on consumed me. I didn't want to upset her, but something held me back. Surely, I could rewind this tape and start again, but how?

"I'm sorry." My apology sounded inadequate even to me.

"No worries. I get it."

I wanted to shout, *No you don't get it at all. I'm not usually this easy and it's been a long time since I've been in the market. I'm not a hopeless flirt who goes around leading unsuspecting women on only to back out at the last second.* I mean, who goes off to a secluded spot with a hot woman she has no intentions of fucking? I bit my lip, preferring that pain to chastising myself another second.

We drove the rest of the way in a dreadful silence until I was ready to press my foot over hers on the accelerator just to speed up in order to get the ride back over with. The tight muscles in her jaw gave her a more rugged appearance each time I dared to glance across at the driver's side. I couldn't stop stealing glances. I didn't want to, but my natural inclination was that this was just so damn backward.

It was just as well I stopped us before we got carried away.

I wasn't looking for a long distance relationship. Faith left me with a big enough hole in my heart without adding an ocean to the depth of my pain. What if I actually fell for this woman? Then what? Who would relocate? Or would we just commute—an idea I found intolerable. Living on separate continents didn't exactly make for an easy way to spend time with the one you wanted to be with. There sure was a whole lot of water between us, not to mention, the obvious differences in our cultures, figures of speech, food, perspectives, the list was endless. The moment Robin had us back at the hotel, I stalked off without saying anything to catch the tail end of the icebreaker. I was absently piling finger food on a plate when Debs strode over in a huff. "Where were you? The organizer, you know, Rachel Smith, grilled me for an hour on our protocol changes. I could have used your input."

"I'm sure you handled it just fine, Debs."

"Actually, I did," she gloated. "Thank you, oh my, there's Kirk from California—a bronzed blonde god. He is hot. He says he used to surf back in the day when his clueless youth supposedly had him doing all sorts of stupid stunts."

"How old is he? He can't be much older than us."

"He's in his fifties, I think, but he sure doesn't look it. I wouldn't mind seeing him on top of a board without trunks."

"On top of a broad without trunks? That's disgusting, Deborah."

"I said 'board.'" She smiled, and leaned into me to whisper, "Where is your head, Janalyn? You're mind seems a million miles away."

"I'm sorry, Debs, can you repeat what you just said?" I had an overwhelming desire to get out of there, call it a night because I couldn't concentrate on anything but my misgivings. I was there to work but found it impossible to get what had happened with Robin out of my head. I had to get back on track. I had to stop this nonsense. I was much too old for a schoolgirl crush and too proud for a mindless fling. I wouldn't lower my standards. Not even for an influential woman with great lips.

"Too bad he lives so far away."

"Tell me about it." I sighed, at once remembering Robin's kiss.

"Wait. Don't tell me you're switching teams? Hands off alert: I saw him first."

"No way, my lesbian card never expires. He's all yours."

She breathed a sigh of relief and followed my gaze, which was planted on Robin, now engaged in a lively discussion with a gorgeous Swedish-looking woman who was touching Robin in a way bordering on obscene and whom I suddenly wanted to beat with a stick. I couldn't ever remember feeling this possessive of Faith. What was happening to me?

Debs grabbed my arm and nodded in Robin's direction. "If she were my type, I'd be all over her and not standing here with me."

"Do *not* go there," I said.

"Why? Are you considering a life of celibacy?"

"Let's just say she is way too much for me at this point."

Debs eyed me suspiciously. "Where were you for the past hour or so?" She pinched my arm. "Do tell."

"Ow. There's nothing to tell."

"I'll get it out of you. I always do."

"Hrmpfff. That reminds me, I need to pee. Catch you later." I walked off and headed out of the banquet room. I could not stand another second watching Robin and Ms. Touchy-Feely carrying on like it was anybody's business. What ever happened to professionalism? Why did I even care? I certainly let Robin know I was off limits, so now that I was done with her, why was I riddled with jealousy? I strode to the elevator and fumed all the way up to my floor and remained irritated all the way back down again, when my keycard didn't work.

How on earth did they design an automobile that started with a key in the ignition or by remote control when they couldn't perfect a simple room key? Back up at my room, I chucked my clothes and headed for a scalding hot shower, but I was seething. Lowering the water temperature and raising the pressure of the showerhead, I endured the discomfort of a cold pulsing jet spray pounding at my naked flesh while replaying nightjarring with Robin and how badly my body had betrayed me over and over again. At least I had resisted the urge for a one-night stand. Two points scored for virtue and another two for fortitude. But did I totally miss my opportunity here? I was determined to put it out of my head, to lay Robin's perfect body and infectious naughty grin to rest in my mind, and just wake up the next day with a clean slate.

I practically beat the feathers right out of my pillow as I tried to get comfortable and watched some fluff float around. I tried to catch a feather but missed by a mile when the air movement caused by my hand propelled it too far away. Just as Robin seemed to me now. Light years away. I dreaded to think how I'd feel if I couldn't bear to leave her and vowed not to let it get to that point no matter what. But I couldn't stop this strong urge, to the point of insistent ache, knowing I was too sexed up to sleep if I didn't come. With Debs out until I had no idea when, I toyed with the idea of indulging in a bit of vibrator play, but after all that tossing and turning, I could not summon up the motivation to move. It was going to be a long night.

Chapter 9

IT TOOK ME HOURS TO fall asleep that night and seconds to be catapulted into action the next morning, when an urgent knocking at the door echoed in my pounding head, and I had to get up to stop all the racket. The room was still dark with the blackout shades and drapes closed. Debs's bed remained untouched. I guessed she'd spent the night with Kirk. The door practically rattled as I dragged myself out of bed.

"I'm coming, coming." I felt like death warmed over, not exactly an ideal look for when I opened the door, and who should be standing there but Robin? My hand shot up to the bird nest that was most likely my hairstyle du jour. "What time is it? Wait! What are you doing here?"

"It's eight thirty. When you didn't come down for breakfast, I thought I'd knock you up."

"Excuse me? Knock me up?" I laughed my head off.

"I thought I'd come on up to check on you."

She had a dessert plate in her hand. "It's a peace offering for the way I behaved last night. There was only one cinnamon bun left. I thought you might like it."

"Sweet, but I'm so late."

"Here, take it. You'll be hungry otherwise." Robin held out the offering. Her hopeful grin melted me all over again.

"That's very kind, but how did you find me? I mean, I thought they kept room numbers confidential. I may call and give them a piece of my mind."

"No need, your friend Deborah, I think that's her name, she sent me to see what was taking you so long."

"She did, did she? She's in big trouble."

"Go easy on her. I have an arsenal filled with powers of persuasion that are too hard to resist." She stepped closer into the room in order to allow the cleaner to pass with her cart. I stood totally dumbstruck, unable to stop Robin from entering. How embarrassing when I remembered all I had on was a T-shirt and panties, and my teeth weren't brushed! My body went into flight or fight mode, at once self-conscious to be seen this way. I could bark at her to back off or slam the door in her face, but neither scenario fit with the way I was blatantly being checked out and how completely I was enjoying it. It was as if my entire body was alight with raging hormones until every heightened sense intensified, clouding my judgment. Only temporarily, as I pulled my thoughts away from my sex-starved body.

"Look, I need to wash up," I said. Her gaze lingered on my bare legs until heat radiated to my cheeks like I had flaming torches set at my feet. I either had to push her out the door or succumb to going up in flames. That's all there was to it. I made my decision and stuck with it. "And you need to leave."

"Can do," she said. "But first, take this." She held out the delectable offering, and no amount of willpower could keep me from accepting her gift. Our hands brushed briefly, too briefly, when she added, her voice low and deep, "I'll see you downstairs. I saved you a seat."

I cleared my throat. "Thank you, but you really didn't have to go out of your way."

"It's my pleasure."

I closed the door, mouthing, "I'll bet." Debs was going to get a serious talking-to. I didn't meddle in her private affairs—much. Okay, so I was there for her through the awful breakup of her marriage and she lent me a shoulder to cry on when Faith declined my marriage proposal, but this was different. I took a bite of the cinnamon bun. "Oh my God but this is yummy," I said aloud.

After I polished it off, licked my lips and fingers, I caught a glimpse in the mirror and was horrified at my reflection. How mortifying to have been seen this way. The bags under my eyes could pack enough clothes for two conventions in more than one climate. And my hair, ugh. Have I ever mentioned how much I hate my hair? The thick wiry mess was often impossible to get a brush through. This time, I used an entire bottle of conditioner and landed a more presentable self in the lecture hall somewhat decent some twenty-five minutes later. It was the quickest shower and blow-dry in history. I even skipped the elevators and ran down the stairs, thanking my lucky stars that there was a break between lectures with lots of hustle and bustle of changing rooms, networking, and such.

Entering the prime gathering area with the buffet at the back, I looked around. My first thought was what happened to that Swedish woman Robin flirted with from the previous evening? Maybe she had been kidnapped by fairies who intended to feed her to a nasty dragon. I could only hope. I glanced at the clock on my cell and groaned before getting a move on. I helped myself to tea from the back of the lecture hall sporting the topic I was interested in. After I added a dollop of milk to the fragrant brew, I said aloud to no one in particular, "Not bad. Not bad at all. I could honestly get into tea."

"We invented it," Robin said. Good thing for the saucer, or I'd have spilled my drink on my blazer.

"Tea plants originated in India or China, not Great Britain," I informed her.

"Yeah, but, it was a Scottish botanist Robert Fortune who introduced tea from China to India and was responsible for bringing the plant here. We've had tea long before America was discovered. The English know their tea."

"Duly noted." I drank the perfect brew as a truce, hoping she would continue talking, but she fell silent. "Have I missed much in the first lecture?" I asked eventually.

"Not really. It was an impromptu panel discussion to compare notes. Those represented included: America, minus you of course, but your colleague and the California team were spot on; representatives from Germany, Sweden, the UK, and the Netherlands all had a lot to add. It was interesting."

"I'm sorry I missed it," I said. The silence fell upon us again, and the longer it lasted, the more I couldn't resist my desire to keep her near me and away from the pawing woman of the day before.

"Where is the woman you were chatting up last night?" I hadn't meant to sound snotty but tossing and turning all night had taken its toll.

Of all the bad luck! Ms. Touchy-feely sauntered over. Did she have to walk like 'provocative' was her middle name?

"There you are," she gushed at Robin. Her accent was indeed Nordic. "Care to join me for dinner tonight?"

She hadn't even given me a glance sideways as she towered over us, all six feet tall, blond, fair skinned and blue eyed, like she knew she was gorgeous and didn't care whose space she invaded. If she stood any closer to Robin, she could have crawled into her pants and taken up permanent residence. This pissed me off to no end.

I didn't know what to expect, but Robin shot me an apologetic look. Was that a question in her eyes? I read it that way.

"Thanks for the invite, Lena."

So, they were on a first-name basis. I wonder what else Robin knew about her.

"Why don't you join us, Jan, and bring Deborah along too," Robin said.

Lena looked like she choked on a hairball. I know the look of a possessive dyke, and Lena sported it in spades. Exactly how much claim did Lena have staked on Robin?

I faltered, but managed to say, "I'll see what Deborah, I mean, she prefers Debs, has in mind later and let you know."

Did I really want to watch Lena play the mating game with Robin? I should think not, but really, didn't I make it clear that I was not in Robin's market when she was obviously on the make?

I worked my way through the crowd and spotted Debs deep in discussion with Kirk. They made a lovely couple. It seemed sparks were flying there, and I didn't want to get in the way, so I went back and accepted Lena's invite. I couldn't let Robin go unescorted, now could I?

The day was flying by. I was passionate about all the topics covered. It was encouraging how well the delegates were getting along. Just before my own presentation was due, I thought I'd empty the entire contents of my nervous stomach one way or the other. But I couldn't very well spend too much time in the ladies' room with Debs knocking on the stall every five seconds. The thought of Robin sitting in the audience gave new meaning to stage fright.

"Okay," Debs said, trying her best to reassure me. "You've got this memorized, polished, and you're going to be great. Hear me?"

"I can't."

"You can and you will." She massaged the tight knot between my shoulder blades, slapped me on the shoulder. "Let's go!"

With her hand tightly gripping mine, I had no choice but to follow. Robin looked up at me and smiled. I took a last deep breath and turned to my first slide. Quite miraculously, once I started speaking at the podium, I was able to relax. By then, I had spoken privately with many who were seated in front of me. By the very last slide, I did myself, Debs and Scott Spencer Enterprises proud. There was applause. I was floored. It wasn't unusual for Robin to receive such appreciation, but I was just a representative from New York without a doctorate and a loyal following. Apparently those in the audience who clapped knew something I didn't. Debs shot me two thumbs up, and I mouthed *thank you*.

During the question-and-answer session, it was Robin who publicly thanked me for the impressive outline for planning the strategies I hoped to put in place with everyone on board. My heart rate sped up when Robin held her arm high in a sea of raised hands. Naturally, I called on her first.

"I'd like to volunteer for the task force you've designed. To do what I can from this end."

I was truly touched, if she meant what she said. Maybe my voice squeaked a little, but I was able to reply, "That would be perfect," before fielding more questions. I was immensely relieved when it was over and definitely pleased with my performance. I intended to thank Fern for coaching me when I got back to the office. Not that I was in any hurry to head home.

The moment I stepped down Debs gave my arm a tight squeeze. "You got the big Dr. Robin Wright's seal of approval. Good work!"

"Thanks, Debs. You deserve credit too, you know."

"Let's hope the rest of what we have to present goes as well. I'm so proud of you Miss Jacobs. So damn proud."

"And I you."

I could just imagine Patrick coming up behind us saying something like, "okay you two, enough with the love fest." I couldn't wait to e-mail him and everyone back home my report.

"If Marcus were here," Debs said, "he'd give you a raise."

"Stop. Let's get to the next meeting."

The topics throughout the rest of the day held my undivided attention, but the moment we were in between sessions, I was forced to watch Lena sweet-talk Robin until I thought I'd go into diabetic ketoacidosis. I tried not to let it spoil my good mood after a successful first presentation, but the distraction of Lena coming on to Robin during each break got so bad that Debs had to repeat what she said three times, and I still couldn't recall one thing I'd heard the entire time. She finally gave up on me as we entered the Torbay Suite meeting room. It was the last talk of the day, the wrap up, and interested or not, it was getting harder for most of us to maintain peak concentration levels. I suspected many were already wondering what they were eating for dinner and where they wanted to spend their evening off.

"Don't you think the schedule is one hour too long for one day?" I overheard someone say. I was about to say I couldn't agree more, but I was caught off guard when I got to the only empty seat left and saw that Robin was to sit between me and that bimbo Lena! I blamed Debs, who gave up her seat to be with Kirk.

Lena leaned over Robin, practically sitting in her lap, with her hand firmly planted on a well-muscled thigh, when she asked me, "What is Jan short for, Janet?"

"Janalyn." If I had said it any more pointedly, I might have gotten in trouble for carrying a dangerous weapon on the premises.

"I knew a Czech girl named Janalyn. Never an American."

"I'm named after a beloved aunt on my mom's side. That side of the family lived in Poland before the war."

Why did this Lena have to be nice to me when I had my heart set on hating her? Especially when it was obvious she was only getting friendly with me to lean on Robin? Maybe I could stab her with the point of my pen.

"I have family in Sweden and Poland too."

Did I look like someone who cared about her ancestry? It was impossible to deny that she was very nice to look at, but each time Robin appeared to be lost in her glacial blue eyes, I worried that I'd do something totally stupid. It irked me to be behaving so badly, but something about Robin had me out of character. This sucked. I needed air. Without warning, I bumped my way out of the long row of seats, causing a domino effect of attendees to stand in order to let me pass before I reached the terrace doors totally winded.

I pushed the handle on the glass door so swiftly it clanged. The door swooshed open too fast for me to maintain my footing. Robin caught me with a strong arm around my waist, literally saving me from ending up on the floor. I hadn't even realized that she had followed me up out of my chair. It was a pleasant surprise, but her embrace was so intimate, I couldn't stop wanting to kiss her again.

"You seem tense today? Anything I can do to relieve it?" Robin said.

I had to shake her off or I'd kiss her right there. "Are you always this, this, this...rude?" I said.

"How do you mean?"

"Don't play innocent with me, Robin. You've wanted to get into my pants from the moment we shared a scone."

"I thought the feeling was mutual."

"It was, is, but that's beside the point."

"What is the problem then?"

"Who is this 'Lena' to you, huh?"

"Who?"

"Don't act all innocent."

"She's nobody to me, but Jan, I would like you to be."

"Don't be ridiculous. We don't know each other. We have nothing in common. For God's sakes, I live much too far away."

Oh God, I regretted every word I said. Here Robin was being honest, laying it all on the table, and I really wanted to accept it at face value. But I'd spent every moment since

I'd come downstairs being completely jealous of Lena and Robin. What was wrong with me? If I was over Faith, then why would I still be affected by the scars she left when she ripped out my heart? It made no sense. I tried to reason with myself, to accept that while I might get hurt again, it would be okay to take another chance on love. I was stronger now. No matter how frightened I was to take the plunge, being a wimp wasn't really my style.

"But we're both here now—" Robin was pleading. I could see it in her eyes. I couldn't believe she'd ever be reduced to begging. It broke my heart to deny her, but I had self-preservation to think about. I didn't want the first woman I slept with in so many years to be just for sex. Despite all my sexual attraction to Robin, I just couldn't bring myself to do it.

"I don't want a fling, not here, not with you." My words were harsh, but it seemed the only way to make her stop tempting me until I had no choice but to give in.

She looked as if I had struck her. I thought I'd be sick; what had I just done? I'd driven her away. And indeed, she turned to leave. But this was for the best, I told myself.

Right?

Chapter 10

AFTER THE CONFRONTATION WITH ROBIN, I decided a drink was in order. I needed something to calm my nerves. I wasn't a big drinker, but a glass of white sure sounded good right now.

I brushed by Debs's elbow as I headed toward the bar. "Debs, when you get a minute, may I have a word please?"

She was at my side in an instant. "Hey girlie, what's up?"

"Why did you give out our room number?" I fixed my gaze on the bartender. He was busy pouring liquors into tall glasses, immediately making me think of Long Island Iced Teas, and I debated whether or not to have one of those instead. But then it seemed so wrong to drink cold tea in England even if the alcoholic version only resembled tea in color and flavor and didn't have a drop of tea in it.

Debs knew instantly what my question really meant. "She's into you, Janalyn. Why not go with the flow?"

"To what end?" I turned toward Debs, trying to keep my voice calm. "It's not like I'll ever see her again after the conference."

"Big deal. It's time you lightened up and lived a little. Too much work and no play make for a miserable Janalyn. Time to get back in the saddle. Sow your wild oats—"

"Stop with the cheesy metaphors already!" What was the use explaining how I felt when I couldn't fathom my reluctance either? I sighed. "Are we getting a drink or not?" I signaled the bartender. "What do you want?" I asked Debs.

"Sex on the beach."

"Oh brother."

The bartender focused on the next patron, making Debs impatient. "Forget the drinks. Listen, I'm staying the night in Kirk's room, soooooo..."

"So what?"

"So, you'll have the room to yourself, is all I'm saying." Debs winked, to which I just rolled my eyes.

"Is this Kirk worth it?"

"Oh yeah, and if it doesn't lead to something more permanent, c'est la vie! See you later, alligator."

"Wait, what are you and Kirk doing tonight? A bunch of us are going for a curry—" I still couldn't believe I'd accepted the invitation for dinner, but I couldn't let Robin go off alone with that woman, now could I?

"We're ordering room service." Her naughty smile said it all.

Envious of her carefree attitude, I watched as she walked off in search of her latest Prince Charming. Maybe she had a point. Hooking up with Robin would add a saucy tale to this trip.

Although people lingered in the hotel lobby after the day's sessions ended, Robin and I did not cross paths. I know I was certainly avoiding her after our confrontation earlier. So, naturally, I was surprised when, eventually, I felt her voice was in my ear. "Be out front at seven."

"Excuse me?"

"You agreed to a curry."

"Oh, yes, okay. Seven."

Without another word, we both strolled off in opposite directions. Once back in my room, I chucked off my clothes and hit the shower that I hoped would wash off a truckload of conflicting emotions roiling up in my stomach. I hated to go along, but I would suffer worse being out of the loop. It was a no-win situation, but I distracted myself by focusing on what the heck to wear. I doubted anyone was dressing up for curry, so I chose a baby blue polo shirt with cap sleeves, a short denim skirt, and blue-jean colored canvas peep-toed wedge heels that offered a sporty comfort and were my second all-time favorite when I couldn't get away with wearing sneakers.

I had another hour to kill, so I decided to check with the desk clerk about renting a car. It turned out the cars available even had GPS navigators they called Sat Nav. Maybe I would go back to the spot Robin and I had visited and see the nightjars once more before I left. I decided that it really wasn't that scary being there at dusk after all. It would be cool to use the recording device on my phone to monitor the nightjars' calls as a keepsake.

As the clerk drew up the car rental contract, I spotted Robin chatting up yet another woman. Didn't she ever take a time-out? What an insufferable flirt that woman was! Well, fuck her, I wouldn't mind a curry, and perhaps I'd chat up a fine woman myself while I was there. I quickly squared up the rental details for the next day and headed back up to my room in a huff not only to grab a sweater but to take a time out.

When I returned to the lobby, there was no sign of Robin, but Lena assembled me and two others for a short trip to a nearby Indian restaurant that turned out to be within walking distance to the hotel and overlooked the harbor. A long scalloped string of lights lined the sky above the sidewalks, illuminating the bay in a wash of color. Even the drawbridge, streetlamps, and Ferris wheel were illuminated.

Someone asked where the infamous Dr. Wright was. Lena informed us only that Robin would be detained, and I was dying to ask what the emergency was without letting on that I cared.

Lena made the intros, and I added very little to the small talk, all the time fuming that Robin wasn't there and was probably off with the woman I saw earlier. She had some nerve trying to get me into the sack while fucking every other skirt in town.

After a small bite of poppadum I hardly tasted, all the main dishes arrived steaming hot, and otherwise flavorful and enticing, but my appetite had simply vanished. The tikka masalas, rice biryanis and rogan joshes blended into one big mishmash before my eyes. I lost track of the conversation so often the others just forgot I was there. When the check arrived, I threw a twenty pound note into the pile and mumbled farewell, preferring to walk back on my own. They were whispering about me, no doubt about that, but I couldn't care less.

If there was a moon, it went unnoticed, because the air was misty and the sky dark, but the hotel was all aglow with enough lights for a Christmas celebration. Out of the corner of my eye, I spotted a woman all wet and muddy. She wore clunky work boots that swished as she scurried out from the shadows and scooted onto the doormat. She wiped her feet before entering the lobby, and when I caught a glimpse of her profile, I realized it was Robin! That did it! I bet she took that woman I saw her with earlier and fucked her brains out in the wilderness by some lake. My mind conjured up every naughty scenario, but one thing was crystal clear: she was a player of the worst kind. How lucky for me that she hadn't shown up tonight, because I was falling for her, and I really didn't want to land in a pile of shit.

Stopping where I stood, I waited for her to leave my line of vision before making my way back to my lonely hotel room. I wouldn't even have Debs to talk to, which sucked, since wallowing in self-pity was not what I needed before sleep. A good movie would take my mind off her and soothe my hurt ego, maybe.

I couldn't believe she stood me up. And it was not just me but Lena and the others too. Maybe Robin was only as good as her latest conquest. If someone better came along, she just grabbed the chance without as much as a thought about anything but her own satisfaction. I pulled out my diary, the soft Moleskine all rolled up from being shoved in pockets and the pages tattered with details in shorthand. The calendar revealed that I had five more days of seeing Robin around and not being able to act on my true feelings, and then I could go home and get back to my life. Five more days.

Chapter 11

LATER THAT EVENING, I WAS flipping through the TV channels, cursing that there was nothing worth watching besides a *Criminal Minds* episode I'd already seen when Debs popped back into the room, dressed all sparkly to match her cheery disposition.

"There are people downstairs asking for you," she said. I was happy for her glee.

"How goes it with you and Kirk?" I asked instead of asking her who these people were that wanted my attention.

"He's so sweet. Oh Jana, I'm going to miss him so much when we leave."

"Ah, well, you can Skype, e-mail, and text."

Debs flittered about the room collecting a clean bra, lace panties, and stockings. "It won't be the same," she said. She was a girl after my own heart, with her racy unmentionables hidden under professional suits and tomorrow's outfit. All the while she was chattering about all of Kirk's finer attributes until I thought I'd strangle her just to shut her up. It was bad enough I had ruined my chances with Robin and had nobody else I felt like fraternizing with during the long hours of the night. Everyone else was busy having fun in

Devon's nightlife, and I was holed up in a boring room with crap TV, a brain too distracted to read, and a body wanting and waiting for something I refused to do. It would be way too easy to submit to my desires and mostly unsatisfying to indulge in my vibrator.

Debs stopped and gave me a stern glance. "What are you doing later, Janalyn?"

I shrugged.

"Well, you're not staying in here sulking all night, are you?"

"Who says I'm sulking?"

"You don't have to say it." She sat at the foot of my bed and wasn't going to budge until I answered. "What gives?"

"What do you want from me? I'm tired and want to have an early night."

"Bullshit! You were elated after your presentation and even after that, but then something happened. Tell me what's up, or I'll torture it out of you."

I smiled as I involuntarily scooted closer to the headboard, as if distance could really save me. Who was I kidding? Good old Debs was relentless in her tickling; she *would* get it out of me. She wasn't content unless everyone around her was happy, so I attempted a positive attitude for her benefit.

"That's the poorest excuse of a smile I ever saw," she said, slapping my blanketed foot.

"I'm sorry. It's just that this Robin has me all worked up. She's coming onto me and every other prospect within reach. I can't stand to be another tick on her bird list, but I want her. How fucked up is that?"

"Not fucked up at all if you act on your feelings. But you'd better stake your claim and soon, otherwise you'll never know what you missed. Don't let her get away with it, Janalyn. Since when are you such a wimp where territory is concerned?"

"I'm not being a wimp."

"Yes you are. Now get out of this bed, get your ass dressed, go down those stairs, and mark your territory, damn it."

"What? You want me to piss on her leg?"

"If that's what it takes, then yes, pee all over her."

"You're weird."

"Yep."

"I'll see. Now get going. You don't want to leave Kirk alone too long."

"He's such a hottie, you're right. See you tomorrow at breakfast. Be forceful, Janalyn, and you'll be victorious."

"Yes, ma'am." I saluted Debs and threw off the covers before she grabbed her bag. At least she flashed her pearly whites before she left. Somebody ought to be satisfied, so that the evening would not be a total waste. I put the outfit I wore earlier back on, ran a big-toothed comb through my hair, and headed out the door.

As it turned out, the bar was packed with partiers from every nation, no doubt all there for the same reason—networking disguised as socializing. The room buzzed in several different languages and many dialects of English—too many to decipher where each belonged. I always loved the English accent—it sounded posh to my American ears.

Robin was at the bar, and I could tell by the way she raised her eyebrows that she had seen me before I could make a hasty exit. I glared in her direction. Gone were the muddy boots and cargo work pants. Once again, she was all cleaned up. With her hair slicked back, she looked fresh from the shower. She wore an ironed light blue and white poplin boy shirt under a navy blazer, navy chinos, and black shiny loafers. The look suited her well. In one hand, she held a pint of beer; the other, she had shoved deep into her pocket as she leaned against the bar in a blatant *fuck me* stance if ever I saw one, chatting up the ladies while making it obvious she was eyeing me. I ordered a house white and put it on my room tab. One drink would not suffice with the mood I was in. She lifted her pint and I raised my glass of wine in return but stood my ground. If she was really interested, she'd come get me.

So much for bravado, I gulped as she quickly excused herself from the group and headed in my direction. Just to shake off a sudden case of nerves, I took a long sip of the sauvignon. I tried to savor the taste rather than gulp it down and felt every ounce of the liquid warmth.

"Hiya, all right?" She looked a bit preoccupied, whereas moments ago, I had been sure she was confident and carefree by the bar. What was going through her mind?

"Fine, thank you," I said, as crisp as my wine.

"About tonight—"

"What about it? You didn't show. Find yourself something tastier?"

"Not exactly. I'm really sorry about that."

"You apologize a lot. Is that a British thing or just you?"

"I said I was sorry. How about I take you to dinner here tomorrow night? Just us, so I can explain."

"How do I know you'll show?"

"You have my word."

I mulled it over, ordered another glass of wine, and gulped down half of it before I deigned to answer.

"Okay, then. Tomorrow, dinner, but drinks are on you, and I'll have a nice bottle of white please."

"I'll do better than that, I'll buy dinner too." She swallowed the last of her beer and tapped my nearly empty glass. "Can I buy you another?"

"I would, only I'd never get up in the morning if I don't turn in soon."

"I'll walk you to your room."

"That won't be necessary."

"I insist."

We entered the elevator in silence. Her rustic scent mixed with beer drove me wild. I longed for a taste of brew, right off her tongue. Robin reminded me of a devilish dessert I constantly craved but shouldn't have. Who was I kidding by playing coy and hard to get? I was opening my mouth to speak when Robin's lips dove in for a kiss that ended too soon as the elevator opened on my floor.

The way I felt, you'd think I'd just climbed a tower filled with countless steps rather than experienced a brief kiss. I knew if I invited her in, she'd come and so would I, but that nagging feeling of being abandoned strengthened my resolve. I hated that I could not just love 'em and leave 'em the way she and Debs seemed to do. Maybe I had abandonment issues, maybe it was because of what Faith had done to me, but too bad; nobody's perfect.

Suddenly remembering Debs's comment about staking my claim, I giggled.

"What was that for?"

Unable to come up with a suitable response, I kissed her more as we lingered at my door. The hall was empty until the ding of the elevator and muffled voices drowned out the sounds of our smacking lips.

What was I doing here? What about the promise I made to myself about not settling for a fling—especially with a suspected lady-killer? Oh, screw it. Why care about staying safe in matters of the heart when my body was clamoring for the sweet release it craved? Mind over body? In the end, I went with the body. "Maybe we should continue this inside?" I said, before I changed my mind.

I cursed when the key didn't work after two tries. She took it from my trembling fingers and opened the door right away.

Grinning broadly, she handed me the key card.

"Hrmpfff," I muttered. Earlier, Debs had called me a wimp; maybe she was right. I couldn't decide what to do next and sighed with relief when Robin took the lead. There wasn't a part of me not screaming out for her to take me, maybe not all of me, yet, but on some level, I knew that's exactly where we were heading. Why beat around the bush? I giggled again.

"Are you taking the piss?" She was absolutely adorable when she pouted with those irresistible lips.

"The English sure use funny expressions. What do you mean, 'taking the piss'?"

"You know, poking fun, laughing at my expense?"

"Absolutely not. I'm just, well…it's all your fault. You make me nervous, hot, and horny, and it makes me giggle."

There. I'd spelled out the truth, be it a sign of weakness or not, so what did I have to lose? After all, it wouldn't be long before our hook up became a faded memory, right? Or would it? The way she looked at me made me feel like I was the only woman in the world that mattered to her. She cocked her head slightly, seeming to take in all of me, as she reached out to run her fingers through my hair. The sultry way she did it made my whole body tingle. I stood mesmerized under her gaze as her tongue moistened her lips. How did she manage to turn me to putty every time? I hated to think she was placing a spell on me, but I couldn't ignore the intense longing in my heart for something deep and meaningful with her. I was long overdue for meaningful.

"What else makes you giggle?"

I winked in response. A flippant message was not really what I had in mind, but placing unwarranted significance into what was about to happen would surely leave one or both of us with emotional cuts and bruises. I'd had enough emotional scars to know that I didn't want to risk a repeat performance.

I didn't know Robin well enough to make a complete and fair judgment, but somehow, against all evidence, I trusted her anyway. That was the conundrum. But there were more pressing matters that competed for my attention. Namely, my nipples, which stung as they pushed up against the confines of my sheer seamless bra, becoming ever so visible through a stretchy, pastel shirt that was so thin I felt one step away from being totally topless.

With little help hiding my current state of arousal, Robin quickly responded as expected, or more accurately, as I'd hoped. She chucked her blazer on the chair before making her move, and our breasts became acquainted through layers of cotton. I couldn't detect a bra beneath her poplin shirt and became deliriously determined to get her naked. I longed for the feel of her bare breasts against the palms of my hands, but was unwilling to rush the tender moment away. There was no second chance at a first time. Undoing the top two buttons confirmed my suspicion, and I was rewarded with a glimpse of the tops of her rounded breasts. To delay the inevitable, namely, ripping her shirt off, I wrapped my arms around her torso and ran my fingers along her back, trying to calm myself. Each of her muscle fibers relaxed in response to my touch.

Meanwhile, her mouth, lips, and tongue were busy doing magical things to mine. Our warm breath mingled until I couldn't breathe without panting.

"You taste so good," I said, unable to properly enunciate, but she got my drift and kissed me deeper. So soft were her insistent lips that every care ceased to exist. There was only longing, maybe a touch of desperation, but no matter: she did not seem to be in any hurry; neither was I.

She gathered my top at the waist, pulled it out of my skirt, and then grabbed it by the hem. I raised my arms as she slipped the flimsy thing over my head before throwing it aside. The stare she gave me and the way she snaked her fingers underneath my wireless bra made me tremble long before she unhooked my bra and removed the straps one at a time. Her seduction triggered a delicious weakness in my knees, but feeling insatiable, I summoned all my will to remain standing as her fingers explored and worshipped my body.

Next came the belt and then the snap and front zipper of my skirt, until I was only wearing panties, heels and a smile. I kicked off my shoes and shrunk three and a half inches. We would have to lie down soon if I was to do all the things with her I had in mind.

I finished unbuttoning her shirt, and my breath caught at her lovely bare, perky breasts, those darkened nipples hardened to luscious points. She helped me remove the remainder of her clothes until we both stood only in our undies as a last barrier between the bliss we both clearly wanted.

I led her to my hotel bed, and she landed gingerly on top of me, all the while kissing me everywhere. Our murmurs and sensuous sighs became the only sound in the room. It was already better than I had expected, but I hungered for more. Much more. How would I stand it when I had to leave?

The nagging feeling was quickly cast aside when she hooked her thumbs into the waistband of my panties and slid them down my freshly shaven legs.

"Your skin is so soft." She traced her fingers from my breasts to my toes.

I was delighted my primping had not been in vain.

"You have a lovely smile," I said.

"You too." Her liquid eyes penetrated mine, speaking volumes that comforted me. This was much more than raw sex. I couldn't explain it, but we had an instant intimacy, the kind that usually only happens over time, where shyness is abruptly, unexpectedly replaced by boldness, because finally, on one day, your nerves are totally lost to lust.

"I can't decide, but I think this is my favorite part of all," Robin said. She cupped her hand over my bushy mound, snaking just one tentative finger inside the slit, which had the desired effect: I arched my back, and soon she had me gushing desire all over the sheets, crying out for more, and pumping my hips.

She didn't waste another minute as she buried her face in my most intimate places and did wondrous things to my clit until I couldn't hold it in a second longer. I had an amazing orgasm to beat all orgasms. That is, until she made me come again soon afterward, and my legs turned to jelly.

She shimmied herself up my body and peered into my eyes, while slowly using her fingers to circle my clit without touching the tender tip. "Are you okay?" she asked, all concerned one minute and sporting a wide, toothy grin the next. "Should I stop?"

"Yes, no, oh shit, shit, shit, I think I'm coming again!" She breezed her fingers over my clit while using one deeply inserted finger to gently massage my G-spot until I was in the throes of my very first internal orgasm ever. Again I came, so hard this time, I nearly passed out—there were stars in front of my eyes and everything—but luckily I remained conscious: I would have hated to miss such bliss.

There was no question she knew my body better than anyone, including me. This didn't feel like it was the first time we'd made love. She read me with a precision reserved for longtime lovers. I knew I'd miss her touch the moment I left Devon.

When my shivers abated and my trembling stopped, she carefully removed her fingers from my totally sated pussy. If I died then, decidedly, I'd have had the best fuck of my life.

How on earth was I ever going to move a limb again? I was unbelievably worn out, and she still had her underpants on? The thought made me giggle.

Robin flipped over onto her back, whipped off her underwear and proceeded to masturbate herself, coming in two seconds flat.

"Hey," I leaned on my elbows and stared down at her face, resisting my urge to indulge her by gazing at all her other parts. "That is so not fair." I pouted. "I wanted to make you come myself."

"Oh, don't be such a baby. You'll get a chance to touch me, but you'll have to wait a bit for me to recover."

"What if I don't want to?" Did I just whine at her? Oy.

"Fine, then."

"Fine, nothing. Spread your legs," I ordered.

She laughed at my petulance, but it did not stop her from doing as I asked. She was wet and her clit was still engorged.

"How do you want it?"

"You choose."

I hopped out of bed and rummaged through my drawer, tossing all the contents aside until I found my *fuck-me* sock with the condoms, lube, and the trusty vibrator I had packed, just in case I got lucky. Lucky had turned out to be an understatement. Robin watched with utter amusement as I popped the batteries into their slot, ripped open a package of rubbers and covered the toy in a ribbed sheath. I pressed the switch three times and came at her, beaming with total glee.

"That looks like fun." She licked her lips, swollen, moist and alluring; I couldn't help but kiss them over and over again. It didn't matter that I was anxious to get down there and perform magic with my favorite wand. I was about to pour the lube on when I realized she had enough lubrication for a factory.

I loved that she felt so comfortable with me already. Things had changed. I felt a real vibe of trust and affection for her that I was sure would only grow stronger with time. After all, she had trusted me enough to masturbate in front of me. In fact, looking back, I had no idea where she got the nerve, but her confidence filled me up, almost making me weep.

But, tears would have to wait. My attention sharply returned to her sex when she held her lips open so that I had the perfect view and access to her fine pussy. She wasn't shy. I dove in to take a taste of her juices, only to be thoroughly rewarded with hums of pleasure—hers, and mine. On the vibrator's third setting, I toyed with her until she stilled my hand. "Please. If you're planning to torture me, you're succeeding."

"Good!" My frisky nature had surfaced after being silent for so long.

"No, not good. Just a warning: retribution can be a bitch."

"Oh?" I pressed the vibrator button and it went up one speed. I tested the power on the engorged flesh, delighted when her pleasurable murmurs spurred me on. Purposefully, I moved the slick silicone tip around her clit. By the way her hips gyrated ever faster, I could tell I was going to leave a lasting impression.

Keeping the vibrator going with my right hand, I used my left to slip two fingers inside. She was wetter still, and her pussy tightened around my fingers like a warm welcome handshake as she neared orgasm. We did this push-and-pull thing where I was sure she'd force my fingers out, only to draw them back in as she got closer to climax number two. It took a while to get her to the brink again, and this delighted me to no end.

"Don't come yet," I said. "This is just too good."

"Don't worry," she sucked in her breath. "I won't. Now, shush."

"Your clit is huge now, and you're so tight inside; I think it's going to be soon."

"Stop talking."

"What did I say?" I teased.

"Oh God, I'm nearly, oh yeah, I'm...there!"

She came with such force that I moved the vibrator away and just used my fingers to draw out the last spurts, hoping she could have a second and third release. The second climax was tiny, barely a shudder, but by the third, she held her breath, stilled her hips, and left the rest up to me. With everything I had, empowered by her willingness to let me lead, I read her clit as if it came with instructions. Increasing and decreasing in size, staying hard for longer periods until her clit was so full, I feared it'd burst. I must have done something right, because when her third orgasm began, she was barely breathing, hardly moving. With all our concentration on the most wondrous gift of all, she rode out the climax for longer than I thought humanly possible until her whole body shuddered and collapsed in on itself. Afterward, she lay on her back just staring at the ceiling for the longest time.

"Crikey. You are brilliant at using that thing. Must be from tons of practice."

"Ha-ha, hardly."

"Surely you make yourself come."

"I don't usually share those details with someone I just met."

"After the shag we just had, I'd say we're like an old married couple."

"Is that what you say to all the girls?"

"Pardon? I don't know which girls you mean." Her pouty lips slanted upwards despite her best efforts to look offended.

"I beg to differ. You're the biggest flirt in England, and possibly Scotland, Wales and Northern Ireland too." But I spoke with a deliberately playful lilt.

"That's not fair, Jan, and you know it." She tried harder to act all hurt, which resulted in a seriously lopsided smile so funny looking I promptly fell victim to a fit of giggles.

"Well, if the hiking boot fits," I managed to say as I caught my breath.

"Oh?" She let the word drag out suggestively. "What about your handy supply of condoms? Wishful thinking or pre-planning?"

"I'll have you know that condoms are wonderful for penetrating some entrances I'd rather not mention."

She sat upright, the eager expression in her eyes too delicious to ignore.

"What's with the mischievous glint you're sporting there?" I asked with more than a twinkle of my own.

"Oh, just imagining you indulging in anal pleasures suggests you're cooler than I thought."

"Didn't you think I was cool before?" I teased.

"Yes, but this new development sheds new light on your adventurous side, although it's true that you're afraid of nightjarring in the dark."

"I'm not afraid, just sensibly cautious."

"Uh-huh."

"Oh, go on, then. Make fun, but remember retribution is a bitch."

"Touché."

She lay back down, and I snuggled up in the crook of her arm. We must have fallen asleep in that position, because at the first sign of daylight, my body ached, and we were stuck together in post-coital glue. Still, I stared at the wonder of her and counted myself lucky indeed. It was a shame to have to wake her, but I caressed her cheek, all warm and red with sleep, and placed a loving kiss on her lips. Rumblings deep within me already began calling out for more nocturnal delights, but we had sessions to attend, people to meet, and an agenda to get through.

I attempted a third time to rouse her. "Five more minutes, please." She rolled over onto her back, and before I knew what happened, I was enveloped in her strong arms. I marveled at how muscular her upper body was for an academic and wanted to ask her what kind of workout she did, because she was ripped. "Good morning, you."

"Good morning to you too. I'd say you're most definitely awake now. A good sign."

"Let's stay in bed all day."

"I'd love to, believe me, but you know as well as I, we will be missed."

"Shame that." She kissed the top of my head. "You were great last night."

"You're a dynamo! I've never known anyone to come that fiercely before." My hand flew up to cover my mouth. "I can't believe I just said that!"

She laughed. Before she had a chance to make a witty remark, although well deserved, I placed my hand over her mouth instead of mine. She tickled my fingers with her tongue, but I didn't yield. So she flipped me onto my stomach and held me captive. "Let me go," I said, doing my best damsel-in-distress routine.

"You're funny." She bent down and nibbled my ears, which tickled and sent shivers the length of my body.

"I could really get used to this," I said more seriously, "but it's really getting late." I tried to get up, but she held me in place with an enticingly firm grip. "I see you're not going to make this easy."

She groaned. I guessed she was not a morning person.

"One of us needs to go first. Do you want to do the honors?" I asked.

When she didn't budge, I extracted myself from within her grasp and went to wash up.

She joined me in the steamy bathroom wearing last night's outfit, minus the blazer. She had that slung over her shoulder. She was just too cool for school.

"Where are you going?" I asked.

"Back to my room to get properly dressed. Meet you at breakfast?"

"Yes, breakfast." I moved the shower curtain aside.

"Jan?"

"Robin?"

"Thank you for last night," she said.

"My pleasure. See you in a few."

Robin hung back long enough to take one last look at me before she left. In that moment, her intent gaze told me all I needed to know. She was as reluctant to leave as I was to let her go. I had a warm and fuzzy feeling inside. I didn't want it to end.

I sang every happy song I knew as I got ready. The day's lectures promised to be really interesting too.

Chapter 12

MY HEIGHTENED SENSES, ALONG WITH a serious lack of appetite for anything except Robin's body, attention and affection, had me reliving last night's exploits in an endless loop. How could I fall this quickly for a woman I hardly knew, and why did she have to live so far away? If it's true that ninety percent of the things we worry about never happen and the other ten percent we can't change anyway, then why oh why did I constantly worry? This was the question I asked myself whenever I let anxiety get the best of me. As per typical Janalyn-style, when things seemed too good to be true, something dreadful would surely follow. Here I was getting dressed while in the afterglow of the best sex of my life, and I truly feared my contentment wouldn't last. I couldn't keep blaming Faith for this because, what good did it do?

Still, if I was going to make a life with Robin, even if I was getting way ahead of myself here, then I couldn't imagine leaving everything I'd ever known for the uncertainty of a future in another country, nor could I expect the same of her. Realistically, I knew it wasn't as if I didn't speak the language or the culture was totally foreign, but what of my family, my friends, my work, and all the rest of what makes New York my home?

This was crazy. I had to stop thinking so far ahead, but my nature made it hard not to at least entertain the what-ifs. She was not like any other woman I had ever met. Thoughts of never seeing her again consumed me, and I dreamed up every scenario whereupon I could stay. But idealizing my feelings prematurely had gotten me in trouble before. I needed to step back, take it a day at a time, and not jump to conclusions that Robin had the same feelings as I did. I needed to know without a shadow of a doubt that we were on the same page before I gave her my everything. No more, blind faith, pardon the pun. If Robin was my second chance at love, then I was going to seize the moment, but this time, with my eyes wide open. Stop assuming. Stop second-guessing, I told myself. Be open and above all be honest. Ask her what she needs and tell her my needs.

I opened the window and took a refreshing breath of sea air. Between the influence of Torquay, with its breathtaking views, and my positive outlook on life, I knew in my heart everything was going to be okay. I didn't want more than I deserved, but I didn't want to settle either. I left the room to head downstairs for breakfast, reliving our first night together with a smile.

We had made love. What we shared did not feel like a one-night stand at all. I walked off to find her, knowing I couldn't kiss her publicly, but I could tell her with my eyes and body language exactly what was on my mind until we could be alone again.

After our mind-blowing sex, nothing distracted us that entire day—not the conference, the other attendees, nothing. Robin had eyes for only me and me for her. All the women she had looked at before last night might as well have gone home, for all the attention Robin paid them. I secretly rejoiced when Robin blew Lena off.

The meeting rooms were brighter than before, and it wasn't because they changed the wattage of the bulbs. I had the infatuation energy most people would bottle if they could. I breezed through my panel discussion— my input was sound, if not a bit over-the-top optimistic. Debs couldn't stop laughing at me in that teasing way, because she knew what had happened last night. Despite all the excitement of putting plans in place I really believed in, I was getting antsy to be alone with Robin. I needed her touch, I longed for the brush of her lips, the tip of her tongue. I longed for her to consume all of me.

I checked the clock a dozen times. The minutes passed too slowly. By four-thirty, I grew excited and fidgety. Deep in thought, I jumped when I felt her breath on my neck. Then I smiled. I was dying to kiss her. Dying, I tell you!

"Let's skip out early and I'll take you to a pub not far from here where we can be alone," Robin said in my ear.

My relief made me want to follow her wherever she might go. "Really?"

"Sure. You ready?"

I didn't have to think about it at all. "Yes." The last two discussions were okay to miss, but even if they weren't, I was so gaga by then, I couldn't care less.

"How about we meet in the lobby in an hour?" she asked.

"Perfect." A surge of excitement grew within me.

"Wear something sexy."

"I will."

It was torture to part ways, but the fact that I needed time to see if Debs had her little black dress with her helped.

She instantly did a happy dance around our room when I got there and told her the news. "Someone got laid! Someone got laid!" I laughed along as I grasped her shoulders, telling her to quit teasing or else.

"Please, Debs, I need something sexy to wear tonight. Please tell me you have something I can borrow."

"As a matter of fact, I do indeed." She threw me the skimpiest crimson dress I never thought I'd be caught dead in, let alone fit into.

"Don't worry, it stretches." She pulled at the fabric to demonstrate.

"Thank God, because I doubt it'll fit a Barbie Doll."

"Oh, it will fit, and I guarantee Robin will go nuts over your ass in this number."

"You're a lifesaver. Thank you." I hugged Debs, and then let her help me into the dress. I didn't usually wear red, and I certainly didn't own anything as short and tight as the 'glove' she was lending me, but when we stepped over to the full length mirror, I nearly cried. Debs was a miracle worker. She even put my hair up—brushing and fastening it with hairpins and spray until we were both satisfied that I looked great.

"Just a touch of makeup, and you're good to go."

I glanced once more at my reflection and appreciated Debs's handiwork. "Thank you." We air kissed.

"Go get 'em cowgirl," she said. "You look hot, hot, hot. Oh and wear these shoes; I'll wear yours. Tonight's your night."

"I love you, Debs."

"Oh, honey, I love you too. It pleases me to no end to see you happy. She seems so good for you. Is she?"

"Yes. I don't want to jinx it, but last night...well, let's just say, I wouldn't change a thing. I just worry."

"That's nothing new."

"I know, but if she's like Faith, too good to be true, it will kill me."

"If she's like Faith, I'll kill her myself."

"I know I have trust issues, and I want to trust Robin, but she lives in bloody England. How can I hope to make this work?"

Debs patted my shoulder. "One step at a time. First step is to let what's meant to be be. I know that sounds simple, but if she's worth it, and if she thinks you are too, then you will work it out, I promise."

"I was so blind with Faith. The signs were there, but I chose to ignore them." I straightened my body up so I was standing tall. "This time, I'm stronger, smarter and more demanding."

"Yes, you go, girl! You are going to do this right this time. Now, go meet your girl and have a fantastic evening." She hugged me then, and I felt her strength and conviction flow through me.

"You enjoy your night with Kirk too."

"Thank you. We'll talk tomorrow. Love ya," she said and was gone.

I got down to the lobby at exactly 5:29 p.m.

By 5:35, I thought of excuses for her.

By 5:55, I was livid.

Where the hell was she? I had the reception clerk ring her room—no answer. I didn't even have her cell phone number.

What an idiot I was! All those glowing things about Robin I had just told Debs! I felt like such a fool.

Tears sprang to my eyes, but I refused to let them fall.

I asked a few of the attendees milling about the lobby who might know her if they had seen her, but nobody, not even Lena had seen hide or hair of Robin. That's when I began to worry and conjure up every worst case scenario imaginable. I barged up to the reception desk, almost twisting my ankle from teetering on Debs's awful high heels.

"Excuse me, ma'am. Which room is Dr. Robin Wright in?"

"We're not privileged to give out guest information. We strictly adhere to a privacy policy for all our guests without exceptions." The clerk wore heavy foundation that reminded me of my grandma's pancake makeup and fire-engine red lipstick unbecoming a much older woman trying to pass herself off as half her age. Obviously nobody sent her the memo that beehive hairdos were no longer in style.

"You just rang her room. You have proof that we are attending the same conference, otherwise she wouldn't be staying in the block of rooms allocated for our group," I said in desperation. "Can't you please, please, please just tell me the room number? She was supposed to meet me here at five-thirty, and there's been no sign of her. What if she's lying up there unconscious? Or worse?"

She shook her head. No help at all. I tapped my foot impatiently. I wanted to throttle this miserable woman and shout that it's no use trying to be all professional with me when you're clearly convinced I'm up to no good. Like what did she think I was going to do to Robin once I got to her room, hit her with a high heel?

"Surely if this were an emergency, there would be some way to get in touch with her."

"I'm sorry, Miss. We can't help you."

"Well, please try her room again."

I drummed my fingers on the desk while the clerk shot me dirty looks. Still no answer.

"What about her cell phone number?" I asked.

"We don't give out mobile numbers either." The clerk looked past me. "Next."

Without her cell phone or room number, there was nothing I could do but wait, worry, and wonder. Exasperation set in, then anger. What if she stood me up again? Why would she invite me, tell me to dress sexy, and then not show? Was she the type of woman that just got off toying with other people's emotions? That was probably the more likely scenario. Last night had been awesome, perfect even. She compared us to an 'old married couple'—her words. What was that all about? New tears of frustration surfaced. Fuck it, I let them flow.

I was not going to stand around much longer and look like the loser I obviously was. If something bad had happened, then we'd have heard sirens or seen other indications of foul play. No, Robin had used me, plain and simple. Intimacy my ass! It was disconcerting to know that my first impression was more accurate than how I felt in her arms. Her strong arms. Those capable hands. Making me come like there was no tomorrow.

I had to stop tormenting myself. I stormed back over to the front desk, tapping my foot impatiently, when all I really wanted to do was kick something. While I awaited my turn, an idea struck me: I wanted to see the nightjars again before I left. It was a good thing I had filled out all the necessary car rental forms, now that I'd made the biggest pest out of myself with the hotel staff. I needed to get out of here, forget all about that two-timing, unreliable Robin, and spend a quiet evening with friendly birds that made no pretenses, had no agendas, and didn't make empty promises.

"Next!" The desk clerk looked like she wanted an escape route when I charged at her again.

"I rented a car yesterday. Can you please have the valet bring it up in about fifteen minutes?"

She stopped banging on the computer keyboard and looked up pointedly. "Do you have the registration number please?"

"It's Miss Jacobs. Janalyn Jacobs." I quickly retrieved the paperwork out of my handbag and gave her the information before heading back to my room to change. Getting out of Debs's sleeve of a dress was quite the trick. When I had changed into jeans, T-shirt, Keens and a sweatshirt, I scrubbed my face, wiping off every last bit of makeup and wishing to wash away my profound disappointment. I had been used. I felt so cheap allowing myself to fall for her tricks. I tried to cheer myself up, remembering the powerful orgasms we'd shared. I tried to pretend I had used her too, but it was no use. I had fallen hard for her, and for nothing.

I skipped the elevator and shot down the stairs almost as heavy footed as I was heavy hearted. Thankfully, the roads leading to the heathland for the nightjar sightings were not heavily traveled. It was going on half past seven, and there was plenty of time to get there, have a brisk walk, and wait. At least one thing was going my way.

That was until I spotted a car similar to Robin's parked beside the road near a nature reserve owned by the Devon County Council. I pulled up alongside the vehicle to check it out. Sure enough, the silver hummingbird figurine was hanging from the rearview mirror; it had to be hers. What was she doing out here? If we were supposed to meet for dinner tonight, why would she do this? Unless…what if she was like Faith? What if there was someone else? Or what if she had just had a change of heart? My mind raced. It took multiple tries to shift the rental into reverse so I could maneuver the car behind hers and park. Although it was totally unlike me to be anything but protective of a prized possession, I flung my binoculars around my neck. At least there was still some daylight, so they would not be totally useless. I slammed the car door with all my might, which did little to relieve the fury I needed to vent.

The nightjars would have to wait.

I quickly found a marked footpath and marched off in the direction I hoped she had gone. I had no idea what I would say to her when and if I found her in this forested area. What if she wasn't alone? Or what if she was? What would that mean? I tripped over the many visible tree roots, deliberating. It was one thing if a conniving woman skipped out on you to be with another, but it was entirely different to have a woman who leaves you hanging because she can't face you. But whatever the reason, I was going to confront her and let her know exactly how I felt. Stronger, smarter and more demanding—that was what I had told Debs I was now. And damn it, I was going to live up to that, if nothing else.

I was so busy ranting, raving and hating Robin in my head that I almost walked right past the Devon Wildlife Trust sign mapping out the territory and warning dog owners to keep their pets on the lead at all times in order to preserve the sanctity of the nightjar nesting areas—or something to that effect. At least some Brits were considerate of others, unlike Robin. If I ever spoke to her again, I was going to give her a big piece of my mind, that was for sure. And that was a pretty big *if* in my mind, even though I was going deeper into the park to find her.

The path led to a lake. I listened to the waders interacting, calling to each other, as they busily nested. I fought to hold on to my fury, but the ducks and geese lulled me a bit. It was one of the reasons I took up bird-watching. It made me feel one with nature—the order of the world restored. I marveled at how everything worked and at the beauty of it all. Humans were the same as birds, following rituals and interacting with each other, only we probably inflicted more pain on each other than the members of the animal kingdom.

I was so busy ticking off the wonders of nature when the sounds of what could only be an intense struggle grabbed my attention. The angry hissing grew louder and, with it, there was splashing and an unmistakably human voice. I couldn't imagine who would be fighting with a swan. Someone was in trouble.

Although well-worn by hikers, the path was impossible to run on without fear of falling, due to the treacherous uneven terrain. With the echoes and the sounds of my feet crunching over twigs, rocks, and roots, I tripped over one tree root and then another. I used the overhead branches within my reach to steady my descent. The pond came into view: someone was busy wrestling a British swan called the mute swan. The frightened bird flapped and fluttered in distress but to no avail.

At first I wasn't sure if the wrangler was hurting or helping the poor thing, but her clothing was soaked through from interacting with an uncooperative captive. I ran over and blinked several times when I realized the bird rescuer was none other than Robin.

"Is everything okay down there?" I called out. Robin had her arm around the swan while casting about in the water with her free hand. I could see that something was seriously wrong, but had no clue what.

"Jan! Good job you're here. Give me a hand."

"What do you want me to do?" I asked, all flustered.

"Steady on, boy," she said to the swan. "Jan, help me get him out of the water."

I moved closer to the edge and started to wade in.

"Stay there," Robin said. "We won't have a chance at saving him unless he's on land."

I stepped back and waited.

"Drop your bag and take off your binos, then get ready to grab hold of him when I say 'go.'"

I hoped I could pull this off, because at that moment she had my utmost admiration. In a feat befitting Wonder Woman, she secured the swan's shoulders from behind and straddled his back as she guided him to where I stood on the bank. Then she shouted, "Go!"

I helped her drag him out of the water and onto dry land.

"So much for being a mute swan. This poor baby sure is noisy," I commented, mostly to calm my nerves. The swan was busy hissing at Robin, even though she was trying to help.

"Good. I've got him. Now you get the disgorger from my bag."

"Disgorger?"

"The thin metal tool with a cylinder at one end for safely removing fishing hooks. This cheeky bugger has a hook lodged in his throat. If we keep him still, I can get it out without too much damage."

"Oh, right." I sifted through her stuff until she nodded I had selected the correct tool. The disgorger was exactly as she described, but until I watched her use it, I couldn't imagine how it would work.

"Perfect." She took the disgorger from me. "Hold his neck, like this." She demonstrated. "Firm, but not too tight. Don't want to obstruct his airway."

Soon I was soaked from head to foot with muddy water from the struggle. I kept clearing my eyes using my sleeve.

"He might be more difficult to catch if someone else tried and failed to catch him before I got here, so I came as quickly as I could," she said, working on catching her breath, but not letting go of her charge.

Once Robin was planted on top of the swan, he calmed down significantly. This was a trick I don't think I could have mastered even with practice. I wondered what other tricks Robin was capable of. Robin seemed to have sides of her I had never imagined. And now I knew why she had strong arms and a muscular torso.

"Hold his neck straighter. Now, open his beak wide," she said.

I pried open his beak tenderly.

"Use more muscle. You won't hurt him."

"Are you sure?"

"Yes, stay like that for now."

I did. She slipped the disgorger inside the swan's mouth and ran it down the fishing line until she reached the hook and could push it free, leaving no more than a pinprick.

"Oh wow."

She threw the hook and line over to her bag, I guessed to dispose of it properly later. I clapped my hands while we both grinned and sighed with relief. I couldn't stay mad at her after seeing this. The more I thought about it, she didn't have my cell phone number, and I could see now why she didn't stop to ring my room.

"What idiot leaves a hook in the lake in the first place?" I asked. "He could have tried to get it out, since it's still attached to the line."

"The same tosser who lets his dog off the lead, litters wherever he goes, and takes no notice of anyone or anything but himself."

"Too true."

The swan was free. He and his missus took off into the wild blue, with streaks of orange, yellow, and purple yonder. I was so proud of her, I pulled her in for a proper hug. She squeezed me tightly to the vibrant, throbbing sounds of mute swans' wings in flight. We smiled with glee when they landed many feet away from us to nest across the pond.

"You've saved the day." I was jubilant.

"Good job you came along when you did. I don't usually get backup, particularly, a competent and lovely helper like you."

"Do you often rescue water fowl?"

Robin rummaged through her bag and took out an oversized towel. She placed it over both our shoulders.

"I'm part of a volunteer rescue team. Although it's unusual to be called out two nights in a row, it happens. There's a phone chain, and I was the first responder available on short notice. When I got the call, naturally I had to dash out straight away, but I hated that I couldn't ring you first. I am truly sorry about that, but there was no time to lose. I'm the nearest one on the team. I was about to radio for help when you miraculously showed up. Lucky that."

"I was so freaking mad at you, but now—"

"Now?"

"Now you're my hero." Shivering like mad all over, I kissed her lips, now blue from the cold.

"Let's say we get out of these wet things?"

"Good idea," I said, between chattering teeth. "Except, I don't have a change of clothes, do you?"

"I have enough for us both, if you don't mind sharing."

We quickly started shedding our clothes before I could be shy. We had made love, so it wasn't like she hadn't seen all of me already. But something about getting naked outdoors not only instilled new yearning for her in me, I suddenly cared what she thought and how she saw me. I suddenly worried about whether or not I measured up to her expectations. One look up into her eyes, and, again, I instantly knew she liked what she saw. She made me feel loved. She made me feel desirable. She was just what my soul needed. "I like what I see too," I said.

"How did you know that I was just thinking about how lovely you look?"

"Because I can just tell."

"I could take you to the rescue center before you leave, if you like?" she said.

"I'd like that very much." So now she was going to show me where she volunteered. Maybe next, I'll get to meet her mother, I thought, cracking myself up.

"Good then. We can head over during a break or just blow off tomorrow's afternoon sessions. It's up to you."

"Let's play it by ear."

"Okay then."

I loved the way she combed her fingers through my hair, moving closer until our bodies met and connected in a fiery kiss that warmed me to the core.

Her voice was husky when she murmured, "We'd better get out of here before I—"

"Not if I don't shag you first." I grinned.

"I see I'm rubbing off on you already."

"You most certainly are, mate."

"You still sound too much like Fran Drescher to pull off that 'mate.'"

"Oh, stop. You sound like, actually, I can't think of who you sound like, but I do like all your sounds." I winked.

Robin half smiled and looked away, appearing uncomfortable about the frank way I had just paid her lovemaking prowess a compliment. "Bloody hell, woman, are you trying to kill me? Please get in the car and try to behave yourself."

I started up my rental and waited for her to pull out first. Soon we were headed back to the hotel, and I wondered whether in my current state of arousal I'd actually leave a watermark on the bucket seat. I was that turned on as I drove behind her car toward the hotel, consumed by one thought and one thought alone.

I could not wait to fuck her.

Chapter 13

"Jan, quick, run: there's Lena and friends." Robin grabbed my hand. With haste, we scurried to the stairwell. "Hope they didn't spot us," she said.

"I think Lena called your name."

"I didn't hear anything." Her tone was arch, playful.

"Neither did I." I smiled, deliriously happy.

"Where should we go?" she asked.

"Debs is spending the night with one of the attendees, a guy named Kirk; let's use my room."

"Have you had tea yet?" she asked.

"I had coffee at the last break before we cut out to change clothes." It was a shame Robin missed seeing me all dressed up, but how the evening turned out so far was much nicer.

"That's not what I meant—have you had a proper evening meal?"

"Oh, you mean, dinner." I saw no point in reminding her that the plan had been to have dinner together—or that I had been much too upset to eat earlier. "Nope, I haven't. You?"

"No time."

Stepping closer, our bodies touching, I clasped my hands behind her neck, stole a quick kiss. The huskiness in my voice surprised me. "We can always order room service, but first I have a better idea." My suggestive smile wasn't lost on her.

"I do as well. Come on."

It wasn't long before Robin and I tumbled onto the bed, tearing off her spare clothes, tossing off all the bedding but the sheets until we had created a cozy love nest.

"You fancy a shower first?" she asked, alternating between nibbling on my ear and taking tiny bites on prickled flesh along my neck, shoulders, and finally, thank God, my breasts.

"No time. Fuck me first, I beg you."

She sucked on a nipple, and I gasped at the current that shot straight down to my clit as she played all over my body with her teeth and tongue. Her knee rested between my legs, and I pumped my hips, rubbing against her leg with greater and greater speed. I caught my last breath just before orgasm, held it, and shuddered from the moment the release started until the very last vestige of bliss. The euphoria, mixed with an emotional release I hadn't been at all prepared for, set me off on a fit of giggles mixed with tears.

"You okay?" Her deep concern etched the subtle lines around her darkened eyes.

I stifled an overwhelming desire for a good cry and peered into her eyes. Again, when things seemed too good, I got a sense of foreboding and a profound feeling of dread; sometimes tears were the unexpected result. She made me so happy in the space of a moment. But could such joy last?

Live in the moment, Janalyn, I could hear Debs say. *Live in the moment.*

Caressing Robin's dear face, I tried to smooth her worries away. "Better than okay. I'm wonderful. Thank you."

"No need to thank me. It's me who should thank you for indulging me. I love watching you come. But why the tears?"

"You've blown me away. Sometimes happy tears just happen out of nowhere."

"Happy is okay then." Robin's sigh was miles better than her frown mere moments ago. Her next statement just clinched it. "You're an amazing lover, know that?"

"In what way?"

"Every way. But to be honest, I've never made a woman cry after sex. What's on your mind?" she asked.

"You. Us. Everything."

"Any chance you can lengthen your stay?"

"I have to get back for more meetings after I've written up all the reports," I said. But I was actually thinking that the longer I stayed, the harder I'd fall for her, and then what? It would be even harder to leave her if I allowed myself the freedom to indulge every emotion and act on every impulse.

"You can stay at my house after the conference," she said. "At least stay the weekend. I can show you the rescue center then, and we won't have to miss anything tomorrow or the closing on Friday. Please, Jan, think about it, yeah?"

I'd gone quiet and when I looked up into her face, I could see how deep her worry lines went. We lived on different continents. We didn't really know each other. All we had was our unmistakable mutual attraction, but were her feelings as strong as mine? Even though she was asking me to stay after knowing me but a few days, she still seemed a bit too independent to settle down with just one woman. I couldn't imagine a strong-willed, self-sufficient woman like her, who could weather any storm totally on her own, needing someone like me in her life. Even if we gave in to allowing a relationship to bloom, we would have to find a way to see each other. How many times a year could we possibly take a vacation together, afford the airfare, hotels, stay at each other's homes? Or attend the same conference? I suspected it would take a lot of compromises to make it work.

She tapped my forehead. "What's going on in there?"

"Oh God. I'm getting way ahead of myself here. I have this annoying habit of 'future-tripping,' where I worry and obsess about the future instead of enjoying the present. I'm sorry, where were we?" I kissed her, hoping to end my introspection before I let it all hang out, and she learned prematurely how seriously I felt about her, in case she wasn't ready.

She placed her hand under my chin and turned my face up toward hers. "Jan? Where did you go?"

"I'm here," I murmured, almost thumping her chest to indicate what I truly desired: to be ensconced, securely settled in her heart. But I didn't want to scare her off. And I sure didn't want this to end after my flight back to New York.

As if we knew that our time might well be limited, once our heavy conversation died down, Robin and I soon found ourselves inside each other's arms again, cuddling and stroking each other's naked bodies on the bed.

"This time, let's take it slower, yeah?" Robin's fingers were back tweaking my nipples. With the other hand, she produced a delicious tingling in my clit as it again rose to the demands her fingers were asking of it.

"Yeah," I said. The ache of missing her seemed already real, even in the middle of foreplay. I felt new tears course down my cheeks. It was just like me to spoil a moment instead of enjoying all that I had.

"What's wrong now?" she said kindly, withdrawing her fingers and watching my eyes. I appreciated her patience, because at that point I was losing patience with *myself* about being unable to control the waterworks. What had gotten into me? I was not a crybaby, never was, so why start now?

"Nothing," I said. "Please, Robin, please don't stop what you're doing. Promise you won't stop."

"I promise, but—"

"No 'buts', now, please."

She cupped my bottom with her palms.

"Well, that kind of butt is okay," I said, the banter back in my voice.

"You have the loveliest bum in the whole world."

"You're just saying that 'cause it's true," I said.

"Cheeky bugger."

It wasn't long before our bodies joined in a series of high-flying feats like birds mating in flight. It was impossible to tell where her limbs and lips ended and mine began. We spent uncounted hours pleasing each other enough to last a lifetime — a lifetime together we wouldn't have. Eventually, the demands of nature kicked in, and our rumbling tummies started a conversation with each other.

"Was that your tummy or mine?" I asked while lazily tracing my finger in circles around her belly button.

"I have no idea, but maybe we should listen to our other physiological needs besides sex."

"What, and move? Oh no, I'm way too comfy."

"Me too, but it won't help if we pass out. Rescuing a swan uses up a load of energy."

"Good point. When's the last time you ate anything?"

"I can't remember."

"Neither can I." I shot up out of bed.

"Where are you going?"

"To scrounge around for a nosh."

"A nosh? Now you're sounding like The Nanny again, *Fran*." She sat up in bed, her breasts beckoning me, but I had to resist.

"Stop. I'm not your Nanny," I teased as I rummaged through the tiny fridge, holding up each item as I called it off.

"Now, don't get too excited: we have one apple with two bruises, a half-eaten Snicker's bar, and two samples of UHT soy milk, in case we're really desperate."

"I'll pass," she said with a groan. "Where's the menu card?"

The room was such a mess it took a while before I found it under a pile of dirty laundry.

"Ooooo, let's order an English breakfast, poached or fried eggs, sausage, bacon, fried mushrooms, baked beans, grilled tomato, black pudding and toast," I read aloud. "Yummy, and fattening."

"What happened to choosing foods wisely?" She twisted her lips in an overdone look of reproach. "Have you forgotten the message of your big presentation already?"

"I could get the eggs poached and have the toast without butter, I guess. Besides, dearest, we did a *mitzvah* today. We earned some extra calories."

"What's a mik-vah?" Her mispronunciation cracked me up. I was tempted to explain that a *Mikvah* was the ritual bath and cleansing amongst Orthodox Jewish women after menstruation, but was too hungry to get into a full Rabbinical discussion. *Food first*, I thought.

"*Mitzvah*, not *Mikvah*. It's a commandment that means doing a good deed. It's Hebrew," I said. "We saved a swan from certain death today."

"In that case, an English breakfast it is."

I called room service to place our order. While on the line, I relayed the operator's questions, "White toast or brown?"

"Brown, please. Fried eggs, bacon, no black pudding..."

"What is black pudding?"

"Stuffed sausages made with pig's blood, onions, oats...."

"That's disgusting. I'll have yogurt and stewed fruit," I said before thanking the woman on the phone and hanging up.

"Come here, please," Robin said after I had put down the phone.

"What for?"

"So I can poke fun at your funny expressions and nasal voice."

I scowled. "No way!"

"I have a very special cuddle for you," she said.

She was irresistible. I still didn't know how I was going to leave her in a few days. "That, my dear," I said, "I can't refuse."

"How long do we have before they bring the food?" She raised her eyebrows suggestively.

I looked over at the clock on the small desk the hotel had provided. "Thirty minutes at the earliest."

"Plenty of time for a cuddle." She graced me with a wide smile.

"But not long enough. I leave the day after tomorrow."

"I know, let's not spoil it." As I walked over and sat next to her on the bed, she reached out her arm and pulled me into an embrace. I snuggled far too eagerly into the crook of her elbow.

I had to be realistic. There would be no plans or promises when I left. Why did she have to be so damn irresistible anyhow? The long kiss she gave me was so slow, deliberate, and sweet. Our eyes remained open, as if memorizing each pore to keep this memory alive.

She said she loved me, and I believed her. But once we were out of each other's sight, how long would it be before she forgot all about me? I already knew I would never forget her. Our bodies melded. We were different enough to keep things interesting, and yet, there was still so much I longed to know about her. We had many things left to share, left to discover about one another.

"Maybe we should get some clothes on before room service arrives," Robin said.

"Why don't you shower first?"

"We might have enough time to shower together if we hurry?"

"Oooooo, sure thing. I'd love to wash your back."

"And I can wash your bum."

"Deal."

It was another way to distract ourselves from thinking about the inevitable. We showered quickly, avoiding touching erogenous zones so we wouldn't be distracted from hearing room service.

In fresh clothes, we heard the jingle of a tray in the hall, and when I opened the door, the aroma of English breakfast soon filled the air, starting my stomach growling anew.

"I am so hungry I could eat a horse, and sawdust would probably taste good too."

She rolled her eyes, but like me, as soon as the waiter was tipped and out the door, she piled her plate high, and we ate in companionable silence.

Everything was delicious. My appetite surprised me; so much for cutting down on fat and cholesterol.

"Americans like sweets more than British people."

I looked up from my food to see Robin observing me wiping my plate several times with my toast, slathered with butter and jam.

I shrugged. "We don't eat baked beans and tomatoes for breakfast. I think the differences are what make traveling fun, don't you?"

She nodded, then patted her flat abs. I wondered where she fit all the food she consumed. "I'm stuffed," she said.

"Me too. You sleepy yet?"

"Getting there."

We shed our clothes and hopped on top of the bed with the fresh linens—Debs's bed. But I didn't feel guilty, because she hadn't even slept in it since the first night. The sheets were cool against my feverish flesh. Robin lay on her back while I took up my new favorite position, head resting between her shoulder and her breast, leg draped over the tops of her thighs. This left my arm with the freedom to explore her breasts, tummy, and whatever else I fancied. I didn't remember dozing off, but at some point, sleep must have claimed me, because I awoke to someone shouting, "*Yes!*"

My peaceful slumber, broken, I nearly knocked Robin out of our love nest as I bolted upright, heart hammering in my chest. Thankfully, she had pulled the quilt up to cover our nakedness at the intrusion.

"Debs! You're back early." I managed to keep my voice sounding pleasantly surprised, but Debs wasn't fooled.

"Sorry, guys. I didn't think you were still here. There was no security lock or *Do Not Disturb* sign. I just came up here for those damn leaflets I schlepped all the way from New York." She shielded her eyes to give us some semblance of privacy, but I could see from the grin between her fingers how pleased she was that I had hooked up with Robin. "It's first break, you know," she told me with a slightly reproachful tone, but only just slightly. Barely a moment later, she winked at me conspiratorially.

"Oh shit! I'm late again," I said. "This is so not like me!"

Debs helped herself to a leftover piece of toast from our room service cart. "The morning session was terrific. I took notes and saved you some neat handouts." She happily grabbed what she had come back for and waved the leaflets in the air. "Can't believe I forgot these babies. There's no way I'm taking them all the way back home. Well, lover girls, I'll leave you two to get dressed. We can't have you creating quite a stir showing up in your birthday suits, now can we?" She laughed at her own joke. She scrutinized the disaster area of both beds and the array of clothes we had left strewn about. "My, but this room has seen better days…"

I love Debs to pieces, but if I hadn't been naked, I'd have gotten out of bed and pushed her out the door.

"Right. Janalyn, don't you forget my presentation is at one, or I might never forgive you." She winked again. Was she warning me or letting me know that she wouldn't be coming back to the room and interrupting us until long after one? With Debs it was hard to tell.

The moment the door closed, Robin flopped back down onto the pillow. "That was awkward."

"I'll say. We should go."

"Five more minutes, please," she said, lightly caressing the curve of my arm, leaving goose bumps galore.

"No way. If we start that again we'll never leave."

"Oh, you're right."

Robin dressed quickly and planted a kiss on my forehead before heading to her own room to prepare for the day. As the conference wore on, we sat together at lectures and meetings. Robin had a meeting with the FDA about legislating bans on adulterating our food supply with unnecessary additives that had potential side effects. Meanwhile, Debs and I worked with a private group setting up conference calls at convenient times, as the time zone issue made it difficult.

"We will have to take turns speaking after business hours," I said. Everyone agreed it was the only way to get us all together.

With that settled, I lead the group in coming up with strategies, Debs was in charge of keeping track of who was responsible for what, and by the end of the hour, I was not only satisfied with the progress, but soon I'd be with Robin again...and I could not wait!

If these brief absences were painful, how in the world was I supposed to manage long periods of time when we would be so far away from each other? I gathered up my extra pamphlets, pens, and notebook and left the room. I searched the masses, said hi to a few, and hurried to find Robin. The moment I saw her walking toward me, my smitten state accelerated until I was somewhere close to heaven, with high hopes I'd never come back to Earth. She looked so incredible

I could eat her up. The swagger, the confident smile, and the carefree attitude that she could do whatever she set out to do. Between that and her handsome, rugged features, I had eyes for her alone. I was tempted to blow off the rest of the day and do nothing but be with her, but niggles of guilt reared their ugly heads. That's not what I was there for, and I bloody well knew it.

Wait. Did I just think *bloody*? *Really, Janalyn?* I was already assimilating the lingo in my mind. It's like I was already halfway a resident. Was Robin already a part of my life I could not live without?

I had never been this distracted at a conference in my entire career, and I hoped it didn't come back to bite me in the ass.

Chapter 14

AFTER CATCHING ME ENVELOPED IN Robin's arms, Debs vacated our room for Kirk's, and Robin checked out of her shared room. Her roommate was pleased as punch, and the rumors around the conference were just too delicious not to enjoy. Lena shot me daggers, until I was tempted to gloat in her face. Debs and Kirk were quite inseparable. I was happy for Debs that he at least lived on the same continent.

By Friday, Robin only had to look my way, and my eyes grew misty at the thought that we wouldn't get to see each other again. Marcus Spencer hadn't returned my call or my e-mail request for an extension, so I wasn't even sure we'd have the weekend together. Yet Robin kept rehearsing our ever-changing itinerary: We'd visit Devon's coastline, the moorlands, and all the most notable castles and pubs. She insisted on paying the airline flight reservation changing fee, promised to feed me, and promised she'd cart me all over the place to fill in my bird tick-list.

I sipped another cup of conference coffee and tried not to think about our eventual parting as I watched her hand glide down the day's agenda. "Do you think we'll have time for a shag before the closing session, or should we skip out on it?" Robin said. "Think Deborah will miss us?"

"I can't do any shagging—or sightseeing—until my boss returns my call about staying here longer."

She handed me her Samsung, and I checked my e-mail. There it was, in disappointing black and white.

"Just great," I said. "Mr. Spencer insists I be at work on Monday because the board members are attending our debriefing." I was nearly reduced to tears.

"What a prat," she grumbled as she read the offending text.

"I know, Marcus wrote the same thing to me!" Debs was suddenly at my side.

"You asked him too?"

"Of course, you're not the only one with an original idea. Leave it to Marcus Slave Driver Spencer to call the debriefing on Monday morning! His father would have given us at least a week," Debs said. "Look, why don't we get the gang together for the last meal of the con? It'll take your mind off leaving in the morning."

"Okay." I was so downhearted, Debs attempted to tickle my waist. But I couldn't find a smile anywhere.

Our discussion ended when the lecturer dimmed the lights and started a short film on identifying demographics and geographic areas that needed urgent attention to improve the health lifestyles of the impoverished. I absently noted the questions at hand: *Education is paramount, but will the recommendations be understood? Will the target groups be able to afford to choose foods wisely?* At this point I really didn't care. I was too depressed about having to leave.

Somewhere in the middle of the film, Robin nudged me. *Cheer up*, she mouthed.

I couldn't lose the pout, which is not to say that I tried all that much. After the meeting was over, Robin and I walked out together. The other attendees left us alone. In fact, it was incredible when they parted like the Red Sea, to allow us to pass. If I wasn't so downhearted, I would have hugged them each personally, grateful for the alone time with Robin.

"We can e-mail and Skype," she suggested.

I had no idea how she managed to be so cool about our impending separation. "Are you even remotely sad that we may never see each other after this?" I asked her pointedly.

"I'm sad you're leaving, but while you paint gloom and doom, I prefer to figure out how we *can* see each other again."

"I'm glad one of us is optimistic."

"As I said, in the meantime, we can Skype and stuff."

"Yes." It was barely a murmur.

"Jan, are you going to mope around all day?"

I pouted. "Yes."

She gazed at me with a sidelong, admonishing glance. "And is 'yes' all you ever say?"

"Yes." I finally cracked a smile and felt the faintest hint of the cloud around me lifting. The more I thought about it, the more I refused to spoil our last day. And as I straightened my spine, put my shoulders back, and raised my head, I gave Robin a genuine smile. She was right. We could keep in touch. I needed to adopt her light-a-candle rather than curse-the-darkness outlook, and the sooner the better.

We didn't get to go sightseeing like we'd planned, but we got to pass notes with jovial banter back and forth throughout the panels. We made the most of our break times and then, at night, planned farewell festivities involving everyone.

There were fifteen of us in all at the hotel restaurant for our last supper of the conference. I didn't even know who most of them were or who had invited them all. It was impossible to converse with everyone seated at the long table, which was just as well, since Robin had my undivided attention. When she put her Visa in the pot and handed me back my thirty pounds, I fought the urge to protest, deciding to pay her back in private.

There was a small crowd around the waiter, while people took turns with his credit card machine. As the group began to disperse and exchange goodbyes, it was clear that most were simply moving toward the bar. Robin and I exchanged dubious glances at the prospect of wasting the rest of the evening in public.

We watched as the waiter worked through his crowd of customers. Robin suddenly said, "How about I give you and your friend a lift to the airport tomorrow?"

"I couldn't ask you to get up at four in the morning. We have to be there by six."

"I want to."

I kissed her lightly on the lips. "You're a saint, you know that?"

She ran a sliver of tongue over her lips, gazing at me with faint lust in her eyes. "I just want every moment possible with you before you go, that's all," she said before getting up out of her seat. "Complete self-interest on my part."

While Robin went off to settle the bill, Debs scurried over to my chair and gave me a tight hug, whispering in my ear, "She's a keeper."

"We'll see," I smiled. "And you try not to run your mascara when you say goodbye to Kirk either."

"I'll manage," she said. "Come on. We're going to be fine. It's not like we're saying goodbye to Robin and Kirk forever. Let's be strong."

When Robin and Kirk rejoined us, Debs herded us into a group hug. If the four of us looked like the love struck fools we were, so be it. Robin and I bid Debs and her beau adieu and said a quick goodbye to the others before taking our leave for our last night together. I knew I would not sleep and suspected Robin wouldn't either. The tension between us was palpable.

"Debs looks happier than I've seen her in such a long time," I said idly as we walked back to our room to pack.

"Kirk seems like a nice enough bloke. I hope it works out for them," Robin said.

We spent the rest of the walk in silence, each of us preoccupied. Sorrow threatened to take hold of me. When would I see her again?

In our room, I was blindly placing items into my suitcase, trying to focus on what I'd wear in the morning when her arms encircled me in a warm hug.

"Thank you for a wonderful week."

I turned toward her, wrapped my arms around her waist, and tightened our embrace.

"You're most welcome." I was sure my heart was breaking, and I threw my focus back into packing in order to avoid becoming a humiliating, sobbing mess.

Robin helped me finish. She even managed to fit in all the souvenirs I had bought.

"Shall I place a wakeup call?" she asked me after we were done.

"You can, but I doubt I'll need one."

"Me either."

"I'll miss you." The lump in my throat remained insistent.

"I'll miss you more," she replied. "But first, I want to make love to you, and I don't want us to think about being apart."

I let her help me undress and watched as she cast her clothes aside, knowing I'd never tire of seeing the way she looked back at me.

Initial sweet caresses grew more urgent and forceful. Our bodies fell together into a steady rhythm, resulting in two very sated souls—souls from opposite sides of the pond. Robin twisted a lock of my hair around her finger as she stared into my eyes. "I still can't believe you have to leave tomorrow."

I turned away, unable to bear it. It was official: I would never again leave her without spilling an ocean of tears.

The silence as we rolled our suitcases to the elevators was like a heavy raincloud about to burst.

"I'll always remember this con as the best one ever," I said. My voice broke, and I swallowed back hard to keep from crying.

"Yeah?" A hint of a self-satisfied grin spread over Robin's face. "Why's that?"

"It's where I met you," I said simply.

Seconds before the doors opened, we kissed inside the elevator, as if it were our last, CCTV be damned.

My lips tingled long after I had checked out and settled my rental car bill. As we waited in silence for the valet to bring up Robin's car, I fought the urge to grab her hand and pull her into another embrace. Already I regretted her taking us to the airport. I was really hoping I didn't blubber all the way there, with Debs as witness.

Silent tears slid down Debs's cheeks as she met us at the curb. At least one of us tried to keep a stiff upper lip. I knew if I climbed into the backseat to comfort my friend, Debs and I would keen all the way to Bristol, so I sat in the passenger seat next to Robin. A couple of times on the drive Robin squeezed my knee, as if to reassure me, or maybe herself, that I was okay. The silence that grew as we got closer to the airport became excruciating, but then to break it would be certain doom too, because once I started crying, I wouldn't stop. It was the longest two hours I could remember.

As soon as we were in the building, Debs choked out, "I'll leave you to your goodbyes. Thank you, Robin. Don't be a stranger. I hope we see you again soon."

Debs and Robin exchanged hugs. "See you in there," she told me and left for the check-in desk.

Robin must have noticed the tears burning behind my eyes and my wobbling lip, because she abruptly announced, "It's no bloody use pretending you're brave, you have to believe it first. Come here."

She locked me in a loving embrace as I soaked her shirt with my waterfall of tears.

"Hey, hey," she said, "this is not good-bye forever you know. We'll figure something out. You have my number now. Text when you board, when you land, and when you get home, all right?"

"Okay." I managed a smile between wiping away my tears with my hand and planting one long kiss on her lips, but then I forced myself to turn away and not look back. No matter what I wished could happen, it wasn't like I was going back to the UK anytime soon. We could make optimistic, wishful promises all we liked, but the awful truth that I would never tell Robin was that I wasn't expecting a long-distance relationship to last. Even as the taste of her kiss still lingered on my lips, I started a new file for the symbolic cabinet in my brain, labeling it *Fond Memories Across the Pond*. I deposited there every detail about Robin and me, then closed the folder and shut the cabinet door.

I did genuinely think it was shutting forever.

Chapter 15

FOR THE FIRST FEW MONTHS after we'd parted, our e-mails dripped with longing and sexual innuendos, interspersed with talk about what a good team we had been at the swan rescue and all the silly, joking notes we had shared at the conference. She had taken to greeting me with "Hello, Jam" sometimes when her face would first appear on our Skype calls.

But I found we covered most subjects except for the direction our relationship was headed. The intensity began to fade, and the relationship began to fall into a comfortable pattern of texts, e-mails, and IM chats. I didn't even have her home phone number, just her cell! Some days I felt like all we had were static memories and e-mails. Maybe it was time to move on.

But compared to Robin, nobody interested me in the least. I toiled my butt off at work to fill the emptiness and to ignore the uncertainty gnawing at my gut, and it was like the aftermath of my breakup with Faith all over again. Aside from being up for another promotion and a handsome raise, I didn't have much to show for my private life. If Robin and I missed a day of contact when real life or the time difference got in the way, I'd conjure up every worst case scenario of Robin hooking up with some hot Brit while I maintained total celibacy. I couldn't justify my jealousy when Robin never professed to be mine or vice versa, but that didn't stop me from feeling that way. Some days, I found myself reminded of the long times I spent apart from Faith, supposedly while she was on business trips but actually off leading a double life with her husband. The comparisons only compounded my loneliness, my fear of commitment, and my mistrust, along with worry that I was misreading Robin's intentions as I had done with Faith's.

Debs was getting as fed up with my moping as I was, but she had plans to spend Thanksgiving with Kirk's family in California, a lot more promising than what I had with Robin.

She stood at the end of my desk, peering at me until I finally looked up. "Janalyn, you obviously have to make the first move—take things to the next level. Go to England for Thanksgiving, for God's sakes."

"What? And miss turkey with all the trimmings? They don't even celebrate Thanksgiving. Besides, my mother would never forgive me." Of course I wanted to see Robin. I wanted to spend every moment with her, but it's not like she had extended an invitation.

"Well, then, why not spend Thanksgiving and Chanukah with the family and think about spending Christmas and New Year's in England? What is Robin doing for the holidays? Don't you two discuss anything?" Debs's voice rose high enough to startle nearby birds right out of the trees.

"We talk every day. Well, most days. Actually, today when I logged in, she hadn't written, which is strange. She usually mails before she leaves for work, unless she's traveling."

"Can't you call her?"

"No, I can't call her. It costs a fortune, and besides, she could be in a meeting. The last thing she needs is for her cell phone to go off there."

"Janalyn, that's an excuse, and you know it." I grimaced, but didn't refute it. She shrugged. "Oh well. I have to get back to my desk, which is piled higher than the Empire State."

I sat at my desk in a total trance. Why *hadn't* we talked on the phone in all this time? We instant messaged if we were both free and at home and awake at the same time, but we never actually picked up a phone. We tried Skype a few times, but gave up when the connection never worked properly. Either she was too cheap to try a different broadband connection, or she didn't want to Skype with me.

No. I couldn't keep doing this. If I dwelled on all my doubts, I'd never get anything accomplished at work. I slammed that hypothetical drawer full of memories shut and attacked the unattended file on my desk instead.

It was nearly eleven at night when I finally finished and walked through the front door to my place. By then, I had worked myself into a frenzy. The whole way home, I wrote and rewrote in my head what I'd say to Robin, in an endless loop until I was so nauseous I thought I'd throw up. All I needed was the nerve to let her know how I really felt and accept the consequences if it all turned to shit. I kicked off my shoes, dropped my keys in their designated dish, and headed straight for the computer, ignoring hunger and thirst. I'd made up my mind. I was going to write her an e-mail explaining that while I really enjoyed our banter and would always cherish the fond memories, blah, blah, blah, I couldn't keep hanging on indefinitely and was ready to move on. It wasn't fair to either of us to waste the best years of our lives.

I pressed the icon for my e-mail, my fingers literally trembling. I had over one hundred fifty mails, mostly junk, because I didn't dare check personal e-mails at work with all the surveillance going on there.

I hadn't realized I was holding my breath until I exhaled after seeing *Good News* in the subject header with Robin's e-mail address next to it. Was I really planning to break up with her tonight? Really? Her e-mail with the optimistic heading was the last thing I'd expected.

> *Hiya Jan,*
>
> *Good news! I've decided to attend the next CDC meeting in North Carolina at the end of the month, and I hoped you could meet me there. I've attached my itinerary. Have a look and let me know what you think. You won't have to pay for the hotel or rental car. Miss you, Robin x*
>
> *PS I think Scott Spencer Enterprises should strongly consider sending their own delegate (hint, hint). Don't you?*

She was coming to the States! Robin was coming to this side of the pond! Before checking out my calendar, I opened her flight info and searched cheap airfares. I could not wait for tomorrow to ask my boss for the time off. Better yet, I had to work out how best to plant the seed in Marcus's brain that we were missing a golden opportunity to expand our world health initiative even further by showing our face at the Centers for Disease Control and Prevention meeting. How ideal that would be if he decided to send me. I called Debs at once to get her input on how I could pull this off. I had every body part crossed that I'd not only be in Robin's arms next month—I could not stand the wait—but that I'd also be the new company delegate convening with the CDC.

But first, and in complete Janalyn style, I replied to Robin's e-mail, telling her of my elation at her news. It would be six months, eight days and fifteen hours from our last kiss when she arrived.

I AM SO THERE!!! Miss you too, Jan x

Then I rang Debs.

The next day at work, I lasted four whole minutes after Marcus arrived before lightly tapping on his door.

"What's the big deal, Jacobs?" Marcus said.

"There's a meeting next month that will move Scott Spencer forward in the direction we want. The CDC is holding their annual conference in North Carolina this year; it should not be missed. And *I* should be the one to go." I held my breath.

Marcus's eyes went distant in thought.

"Sure," he said with what sounded like pleased surprise in his voice "Submit a proposal and I'll consider it."

All at once I let out a silent whoop. He hadn't dismissed me! There was hope. Either way, I was going to North Carolina, even if I had to use up all my vacation time. I could have hugged the air out of him with gratitude. Debs took one look at me as I practically skipped my way back to my desk and flashed me two thumbs up.

North Carolina here I come!

I texted Debs so as not to speak in front of our coworkers within earshot. I didn't want to invite competition.

But I mustn't get ahead of myself. He said I should submit a proposal. Whooo freaking whooo.

You've got this! Let me know if you need any help.

Thanks.

It took heroic strength to concentrate long enough until lunch when I could fire up my iPad at a nearby Starbucks and write up a quick proposal. With what I had written, I was sure I couldn't lose. God only knows where this confidence came from, but Robin was already rubbing off on me. I couldn't wait until Marcus gave the go-ahead, although I knew I should. I texted Robin the good news. She acted as excited as I felt.

Drumming my fingers on the desk after I had imbibed more caffeine than my already jittery nerves could take, I waited and wondered and probably drove Debs up a wall when I wouldn't stop shaking my right leg, causing both our cubicles to vibrate. When I thought I'd explode if I didn't do something, Marcus's secretary called me into his office. I bolted up, smoothed out my skirt, and walked in like I owned the space where I stood. At least that's what I silently assured myself in order to still my otherwise shaking limbs. It wasn't the end of the world either way, but with all my being, I wanted this. I didn't mind going there on vacation, but it would be like being a trophy wife to watch Robin work. I liked to think our relationship would start and remain on equal footing. I never wanted to be in the position of putting my partner's needs completely ahead of my own, leaving nothing left of me to fall back on in case things went sour.

"Come in, Jacobs and close the door."

I did and waited a beat. "Sit," he said.

"I've read your proposal and on short notice. I was impressed, but it was your work in Europe that threw the ball in your court. Can you be ready in a month?"

"Yes, sir!"

"Good, I'll have Cynthia put you on the registration and all that."

I didn't dare tell Marcus that I didn't need a hotel room. But I would book a flight *today*. The day was full of surprises, and it was all good.

That evening when I got home, I dropped everything and headed straight for my desktop. I usually turned it off if I was going to be away for more than an hour or so, but that morning, in my haste to speak to my boss, I'd simply forgotten. Now I was glad I only had to jiggle the mouse and voila! There it was: she was still signed onto Facebook. I glanced at the right hand corner of my computer screen— seven fifteen meant quarter past midnight on her side of the pond. She had stayed up past her bedtime.

Hi there! My boss said yes. And get this: I'm going to work too.

Brilliant! Book a flight and send me the details.

Her instant response made my heart race.

I already have.

I then shot her the flight confirmation details in an e-mail.

Got it, thanks. I'm pleased. I'll reserve us a double room, yeah?

Perfect.

Sorry, but must sign off for now, early day tomorrow. Great news though. I'm really happy. Sweet dreams, mate. x.

Me too. Can't wait. Sleep tight. x.

There was a lot to prepare, but I zipped through my PowerPoint preps, designed and ordered leaflets, and wrote two lectures. I only needed one, but it never hurt to have a backup just in case they asked at the spur of the moment.

"You don't even need an airplane," Debs said to me one day when she brought our usual dose of coffee to my cubicle. "You're already flying way above the clouds."

"How cliché," I replied, but I continued glowing like the lighthouse at Robert Moses State Park.

More than one colleague asked me if I'd changed my hairstyle or started working out at the gym, because I looked and felt better than I had in months. Eventually, I realized I had to tone down my enthusiasm, lest I tempt fate. I also feared the six-month gap might make Robin and me shy with each other. It was not like we were strangers after the last conference, and we had continued to be in touch with each other ever since. But still, I was a ruminator from birth and often got lost in needless overthinking, so maybe that's all it was. I've often thought I should take up yoga or needlepoint or something to channel my tendency toward out-of-control fretting into something more constructive.

But her last e-mail before I closed my eyes that night was enough to sustain me:

> *Counting the seconds until we're together again. I miss you more than you know. Sleep well, my lovely. You'll be in my dreams. Night, night. XXX*

Chapter 16

I arrived at Charlotte/Douglas International Airport one hour before Robin and made my way to her terminal. I debated on having a drink first, but excitement at being right at the gate when she arrived won out, and I wheeled my suitcase over, not even stopping at the ladies' room. It had been so long since we last stood on the same ground. I hoped she'd been faithful. I hoped she would be ecstatic to see me; I hoped we wouldn't be awkward; and I hoped I didn't pass out from this full-blown case of nerves. My heart was racing, my stomach flip-flopped, and my mind refused to let me calm down. Maybe a drink would have been a good idea, but by then it was too late. The screen showed she was at the runway. She would be there soon.

Seconds turned into minutes, I cursed Customs, as I knew all about the long lines and endless way they grilled foreigners. I was impatient to see her, to breathe the same air, to touch her. I wanted to hear her voice, to inhale her scent. I wanted my hug already.

When I didn't think I could stand it any longer, there she was, a bit rough, as she called being tired and disheveled, but she was every bit as gorgeous as the day I first set eyes on her.

Her genuine smile, the slight tilt of her head, and confident swagger turned my legs to liquid jelly—just seeing her. Her hair was longer and shaggier than at the conference, which softened her chiseled features, but not enough to diminish her commanding presence.

The moment I saw her, I knew we would be all right. She ambled toward me, because my limbs simply would not work. I could not speak either. It had been too long since I had seen such a welcome sight. I wanted to fling myself into her arms, plant my kisses on her waiting lips, and crawl into her heart, her pants, whatever. But she got to me first, and all I received was a chaste hug. I can't say I blamed her for erring on the side of caution, as North Carolina had plenty of anti-gay legislation, but I did know that I wanted more than a sisterly hug. The moment my brain finished freezing up, I kissed her like I meant it. To my delight, the ice melted, and we both visibly relaxed.

"You look gorgeous," I gushed. All my anxieties about this meeting were rapidly extinguishing.

"I'm rough, but you are more beautiful than I remembered." She took a step back, and the way she peered at me made me tingle all over. "I reserved us a car to the hotel."

"Excellent. I can't wait to get there so I can rip your clothes off."

"I thought we discussed this. Behave yourself," she said, but her body curved in a relaxed, playful way.

"Nonsense," I said, "That was just e-mail babble. Just wait until I get you somewhere private. No behaving then."

She smiled. "I see I'm going to have my hands full."

I beamed from head to toe.

The convention in North Carolina was a huge success. With Robin spurring me on, I was at my professional and personal best. We practiced our presentations; she calmed my nerves with multiple orgasms; and between lovemaking we even had time to talk seriously about our future. I wasn't convinced that there was a future for us on the same continent, but I was bursting to profess my love and undying devotion.

"I already dread leaving," I said.

"Let's not spoil it." She held me then, and I tried hard not to get misty. No such luck.

"Are you crying?"

"Of course not!" I absently used her shirt to dab my eyes before I realized what a mess I'd made. "Oh shit, I've gotten mascara on your top."

"No worries, listen: I've been thinking."

"Should I be worried now?"

"Hear me out, please."

"Go on then."

"I love you, Jan. I have from the moment we met. I thought I was a right nutter when it happened so quickly, but there's no denying we have something here."

The floodgates opened then. "I love you too. I want us to be together, but I don't see how that's possible. I'm up for a promotion and you love your job and what about family, friends—"

"Shhhhhh, one step at a time. We're still in the airport, hey? I love you so much, and if you feel the same, we will figure it out. In the meantime, we can work through the separation. I know it will be hard, but anything worth having is worth working toward. I will wait for as long as it takes to be with you. You mean the world to me."

She gathered me into her arms and I felt at once at home in her embrace. I could hardly believe she would be willing to sacrifice anything for me; this new discovery warmed me to the very core, reassuring me that anything was possible.

"What do you think?" She pulled away and gazed at me with a worried anticipation I hadn't ever expected to see in someone who I always thought of as so accomplished and so sure of herself. Seeing her all flustered was endearing. "You don't have to decide today."

I was tempted to let her go on like that for a while, but my impatience won out. "Robin, dearest, I'm yours." I flung my arms around her neck.

"Whoa, not so tight. Should I take that as a yes?"

"Yes, yes, yes!" I let optimism take over, and I squashed every ounce of doubt before it could deflate my exuberant bubble.

"Don't go back," I said. "Come home with me, please."

She smiled. "I'd like that."

"Really?" I bounced on my heels.

"I'll change my flight. I've never been to New York."

"You're going to love New York City." If elation were enough, I could clear the high jump without a pole.

"I know I will, because I love wherever you are."

"What a charmer I fell in love with." I was smiling myself silly.

"I'm ready for a deluxe tour of the Big Apple."

"I plan to spoil you rotten."

"As you should."

I playfully swatted her arm. I couldn't wait to tell Debs the marvelous news and thought a flashing billboard at Times Square wasn't adequate broadcasting for how exuberant I felt.

I might even introduce her to my parents.

Chapter 17

With exhilaration oozing out of my every pore, I texted Debs the good news.

> *Robin is coming home with me!!!!*
>
> *Most excellent news. We are going to paint the town red. That's if and when you're not too busy fucking like rabbits. So happy for you Janalyn. I'll help with the plans. If I don't have you two married by the weekend, it won't be my fault.*
>
> *Let's not get ahead of ourselves.*
>
> *See you soon. Text the second you land. In the meantime, want me to stock the fridge and wine rack?*
>
> *Would you?*
>
> *Of course!*
>
> *Thanks, sweetie pie. You're the best, talk soon. x.*
>
> *Laters, lover girl. x.*

Debs was the best friend ever.

The moment Robin and I arrived at my door, she put her bags down and confiscated my keys. "Let me do the honors, please."

"With pleasure."

I giggled as she carried me over the threshold. We made love right there on the floor, then christened the couch, and finally employed the kitchen table's hardness to give me knockout orgasms. Afterward, we had a leisurely dinner and finally retreated back to my bedroom where we caught only a few hours of sleep.

Nevertheless, we awoke the next morning refreshed and ready to tackle the sights, sounds and treats of New York City in all its glory. I played "Empire State of Mind" on YouTube to get us excited, and Robin poked fun when I rapped my own rendition of the song. We wasted little time getting ready and heading out for tour day numero uno.

Robin went nuts over finally being in Jay-Z's famed "Concrete Jungle." I'd go so far as to say she acted like a big kid on the ride of her life, at times, which cracked me up. She preferred being deep in the heart of Central Park to Times Square, although she did get a kick out of sampling some local Jewish delicacies as we ate sour pickles right out of the barrel. She was skeptical, but I even finally convinced her to share a matzoh ball soup with me, chopped liver on Melba toast, and pickled herring. I think her favorite, though, were the Hebrew National hot dogs smothered with mustard and fried onions. It was gratifying to introduce her to the foods of my heritage and experience it through her eyes.

Nights were filled with lovemaking, old movies, and then more sex; it's a wonder we could walk, much less stand. Debs joined us for a salad, pizza and wine at our favorite pizzeria until we were drunk out of our heads. In the ladies' room, Debs hugged all the air out of my lungs.

"Janalyn, I have never ever seen you this happy in all the years I've known you. Don't let this one get away no matter what."

"I don't plan to."

"Good girl. Even if I'll miss you terribly if you move away…"

"Who said anything about moving?" I stopped drying my hands, the air stilled, and all grew quiet with the air drier off as I gaped at Debs.

"Don't look so shocked. You never know."

"I'm taking it a day at a time, Debs. I'm a new woman." It was true and to prove it, I puffed out my chest.

"You're that for sure. I'm so proud and happy for you. I love you like the sister I always wished for."

"I love you too, Debs. I've always wanted a sister too. We'll be friends till the end."

I hiccupped.

"You're drunk."

"So are you. Besides I'm just high on life."

"You're corny."

"Horny," I corrected.

Debs laughed. "That too. You two belong together no matter which side of the pond you end up, I expect to have open-ended invitations."

I grimaced. "I'm so sorry Kirk didn't work out."

Debs shrugged. "There's a reason why a guy like him never married. I'm fine with having fond memories of the fun while it lasted."

"You'll meet your mate."

"I know I will, but I have to get you married off first."

"Stop getting ahead here." I squeezed her tight. I was so lucky to have her in my life. And with Robin, I could conquer the world.

"Let's not leave your girlfriend alone a moment longer."

We walked Debs home before going back to my place. It gladdened my heart quadruple-fold that Robin and Debs got along so well, even if I had to bear the brunt of endless teasing from a formidable team. But laughing at my own expense was something I'd never outgrow. And I knew they always had my back.

With our fingers intertwined, our arms swinging freely in a comfortable, familiar way, Robin and I spent the next day walking along the Lower East Side, window-shopping for a leather jacket. Everything with her felt as if we were indulging in a well-planned, hedonistic vacation in paradise. Her firm, yet tender grip transferred amazing strength from her to me. She was the lifeline to a confidence I'd never felt as strongly before.

Robin lifted my hand and brushed my knuckles with her soft lips. "What are you thinking?"

We kept strolling at a delightful leisurely pace, and I turned to glance at her soft relaxed features. She exuded the kind of confidence and calm I always wanted to project. "I'm just thinking about you." The corners of my lips curved upwards. My skin tingled from an inner glow.

"Tell me," Robin said.

"You already know." I smiled.

"Tell me anyhow."

"I love being here with you. I also love being in Devon with you. I have no doubt I will love being anywhere in the world as long as I'm with you."

Robin stopped in the middle of the sidewalk. She pulled me closer to the store fronts so as not to be in the way of people walking by, and without further hesitation, she kissed me with a passion that reached right down to my toes.

When we parted to catch our breath, she threaded her fingers through my hair, looked deep into my eyes, and it was like I could see inside her soul at that very moment. Through thick and thin, I knew instantly that whatever hurdles may stand in our way, we would make this work.

"I love you more than I ever thought possible to love another human being. Sure, I've had lots of puppies I was mad about, but you, Janalyn, you do my head in."

I was overwhelmed, to say the least and kissed her with the deepest of passion. Some guy whistled at our spectacle, and Robin shot him a menacing look as he kept walking.

"Let's get out of here," she said.

"Let's get you one of those sexy leather jackets; maybe they'll have pants to match."

She grinned. "That's a bit much."

I leaned in closely. "I already can't wait to fuck you. Seeing you in leather, well, let's just say, you may never walk again."

Robin chuckled. "Janalyn, Janalyn. Behave yourself."

"With you in leather? Not a chance."

That day was glorious. By the time we finished "window-shopping," Robin needed a new suitcase for all her purchases.

"I'd better get out of here before I have no money left to treat you to lunch. Are you hungry?"

"You've never had a bagel, cream cheese and lox until you've had one in New York City," I said. "You're having one."

"We have those in Devon."

"Not the same. Trust me."

We headed to Russ and Daughters. "I'm taking you to a family-owned appetizing store. It's what New Yorkers call the place where they sell smoked and pickled fish, dairy items like cream cheese and other delicacies that doesn't include beef, pork or poultry, in accordance with Jewish dietary laws. It's been around since the early, early 1900s. It's historical."

"Compared to European establishments—"

"Okay, okay, so it's not that old." I laughed. I hadn't played tour guide in so long, I was having a blast.

"It smells delicious in here," she said when we entered the place.

I took a number at the counter. We could barely stand together in the thick of the crowd standing there, waiting to be served.

"It's a popular place," Robin observed.

"You'll see why soon enough."

"I have no idea what to order."

I squeezed her hand. "Leave it all to me."

When it was our turn, I asked for a half of Gaspé Nova loin cut smoked salmon, white fish, and some pickled herring in cream sauce, some plain with extra onions and curried herring. I wanted to make her feel at home as possible and thought she would appreciate Indian spices. I even got some pickled lox. There was enough choice to tempt a small planet, and my mouth watered to get all the food home. I also bought several different flavored cream cheeses, and all varieties of bagels, bialys and smoked peppered salmon. For dessert I chose a pound of rugelach, some candied fruit, halvah, Medjool dates, and my all-time favorite, chocolate jelly rings. I told her that this last one always reminded me of Grandma and my mother's grandma—her *bubbe*.

"What is a *bialy*?" Robin mispronounced *bialy* so incorrectly, I had to hold my sides to keep my *kishkas* in. "And what's a bubbah?" she added.

"My *bubbe* is my great grandma. And a *bialy* is hard to explain, but I'm going to toast you one with butter and sweet Muenster cheese the way my mother did for me when I was a kid. You'll love it."

"I need something soon. I'm getting peckish."

"We can get a nosh to go and eat it on a bench somewhere."

"Are you going to keep using all these weird words?" she asked.

"I can't help it, being in an appetizing store brings out the best in me."

With freezer packs to hold the goodies till we got home, Robin could not get over the cost, let alone the amount, of food I had bought 'in one go.'

"How are we supposed to eat all this?" she asked.

"Oh, we'll manage."

When we reached the bench outside, I handed her a wrapped everything bagel with plain cream cheese and the best nova, and she hummed blissfully as she chewed. She had a bit of cream cheese at the corner of her mouth, and it gave me a bright idea: I leaned in and licked it off.

"This is *lush*," she murmured.

"Enjoy. And there are so many more treats in store."

"I'll have to buy larger clothes at this rate."

"We can hit the gym. You'll be all right."

She shot me a salacious grin. "Or we can have sex."

My eyebrows raised. "Mm. That too."

We finished the bagels in silence. Talking would only get in the way of this gastronomic pleasure.

I stood up and wiped the crumbs off my dress, I looked across East Houston Street and nearly choked on my spit. I suddenly had to sit down or faint.

Robin looked alarmed. "What is it?"

I coughed, cleared my throat, and soon found a new composure I hadn't thought possible. Across East Houston Street had been Faith coming out of a shop alone. Not a hair on her head had changed in all these years. Perhaps she did look a bit tired from where I sat, but the most startling difference was how little effect she had on me, once I'd gotten over the shock. Gone was any spark of interest. Gone were all the emotions I had harbored about her for years—the anger, the hurt, the love. It hit me that I had felt all these things for a person I really didn't know.

Most surprisingly, I realized that I had absolutely no regrets about it. In fact, I silently thanked Faith for giving me the strength and basis for comparison as I was about to embark on a new and greatly improved relationship with Robin. Faith had done me the greatest favor by making me dump her. I pitied any woman who fell victim to her charms the way I did, but I also knew she'd get hers someday.

I was so over her.

Fueled beyond words, I gave Robin the grandest smile. "Oh, nothing. Just realized what a blessing you are."

"That's a relief. You looked like you were about to choke."

She took most of our packages, while I grabbed what was left off the bench, and without a free hand, we ventured to the subway for the quickest way home, my thoughts only on what ways I could seduce the love of my life over an indoor picnic on my bed.

Waking up with Robin in my bed was bliss. I blinked several times to check that she was really there. She fought not to let me go in the shower, but agreed after my promises to make us a full Russ and Daughters feast. With the lox, eggs and onion ready and warming on plates in the oven at low temperature, I toasted bagels, and then washed the cooking utensils, pans and dishes. Unable to remember all the words from the popular '70s tunes, I sang, "Skippity-do-da," swaying my hips in time to the rhythm in my head. I placed the clean frying pan on the drain board, belting out every song that popped into my mind from Donna Fargo and Karen Carpenter tunes popular in my youth when Robin wrapped her arms around me from behind.

I jumped. "Robin! You scared the bejesus out of me."

"I had no idea you liked to sing and make up your own words. Is there anything else I should know about?"

"I don't think so," I replied. "Except for maybe my middle name is Melody."

"That explains it. I see I'm going to have to get used to jam and song. This is good news since I already have the woman."

That was not the only thing she was going to have to get used to because we'd both have to make adjustments. We couldn't exactly compromise by living in the middle of the ocean, so deciding on who would move would be a major hurdle. Then there would be all the little decisions in between—how often the phone calls would be, where we would celebrate the holidays, when and how we would meet each other's families when they were a plane ride away from each other? The biggest hurdle was: would a long-distance relationship be enough? But being together forever meant visas, sacrifices, commitment, and lifestyle changes for at least her or me. It was all so very complicated and expensive and emotionally risky if it didn't work out.

There was much about being together that would be hard, and there'd be adjustments to make on both our ends.

But we were not going to let a little pond stand in our way.

About Cheri Crystal

Cheri Crystal is a healthcare professional by day and writes erotic romances by night. She was born and raised in New York and lives in the United Kingdom with her wife. Cheri began writing fiction in 2003 after reviewing for *Lambda Book Report*, *Just About Write*, *Independent Gay Writer* and other e-zines. She is the author of *Attractions of the Heart*, a 2010 Golden Crown Literary Winner for lesbian erotica. In her spare time, she enjoys swimming, hiking, viewing wildlife, cooking, jigsaw puzzles and spending quality time with family and friends. Visit www.chericrystal.com and friend her on Facebook for the latest news.

CONNECT WITH CHERI CRYSTAL:
Webseite: www.chericrystal.com
Facebook: www.facebook.com/chericrystal

Other Books from Ylva Publishing

www.ylva-publishing.com

Getting Back

Cindy Rizzo

ISBN: 978-3-95533-395-9
Length: 239 pages (73,000 words)

At her 30th college reunion, Elizabeth must face Ruth, her first love who bowed to family pressure long ago. As they try to reconcile the past, Elizabeth must decide whether she is more distrustful of Ruth or of herself. Is she headed for another fall or does she want to be the one who walks away this time? It's not easy to know the difference between getting back together and getting back.

Once

L.T. Smith

ISBN: 978-3-95533-399-7
Length: 295 pages (77,000 words)

Beth Chambers' life is no fairytale. After four years in a destructive relationship, Beth decides enough is enough and leaves her girlfriend, taking Dudley, her dog, with her. At her lowest point, she meets Amy Fletcher, a woman who appears to have it all–and whom she believes would never want more than friendship. Beth needs to believe in magic once more for her dreams to come true. But can she?

Under a Falling Star

Jae

ISBN: 978-3-95533-238-9
Length: 369 pages (91,000 words)

Falling stars are supposed to be a lucky sign, but not for Austen. The first assignment in her new job—decorating the Christmas tree in the lobby—results in a trip to the ER after Dee, the company's COO, gets hit by the star-shaped tree topper.

There's an instant attraction between them, but Dee is determined not to act on it, especially since Austen has no idea that Dee is her boss.

Coming Home

Lois Cloarec Hart

ISBN: 978-3-95533-064-4
Length: 371 pages (104,000 words)

Rob, a charismatic ex-fighter pilot severely disabled with MS, has been steadfastly cared for by his wife, Jan, for many years. Quite by accident one day, Terry, a young writer/postal carrier, enters their lives and turns it upside down.

Coming from Ylva Publishing

www.ylva-publishing.com

Where the Light Plays

C. Fonseca

Dr. Caitlin Quinn is a sophisticated, self-assured Irish art historian visiting Australia on sabbatical. That doesn't mean she can't enjoy the local scenery–especially sun kissed Surfcoast artist, Andi Rey. Their attraction is unstoppable, but their lives are moving in oppositedirections. Andi doesn't need distractions and a woman that eschews commitment spells trouble, with a capital "T".

Rewriting the Ending

hp tune

A chance meeting in an airport lounge and a shared flight itinerary leaves Juliet and Mia connected. But how do you stay connected when you've only known each other for twenty four hours, are destined for different continents and each have a past to reconcile?

Across the Pond
© 2015 by Cheri Crystal

ISBN: 978-3-95533-387-4

Also available as e-book.

Published by Ylva Publishing, legal entity of Ylva Verlag, e.Kfr.

Ylva Verlag, e.Kfr.
Owner: Astrid Ohletz
Am Kirschgarten 2
65830 Kriftel
Germany

www.ylva-publishing.com

First edition: December 2015

Credits
Edited by Michelle Aguilar
Proofread by Joan Bassler
Cover Design & Printlayout by Streetlight Graphics